FOR HER SON

COLLEEN SMITH-DENNIS

LMH PUBLISHING LIMITED

Editor: Kenisha T. Duff
Cover Illustration: Courtney Lloyd Robinson
Cover Design: Sanya Dockery
Book Design, Layout & Typesetting: Sanya Dockery

Published by LMH Publishing Limited
Suite 10-11, Sagicor Industrial Park
7 Norman Road
Kingston C.S.O., Jamaica
Tel.: (876) 938-0005; 938-0712
Fax: (876) 759-8752
Email: lmhbookpublishing@cwjamaica.com
Website: www.lmhpublishing.com

Printed in the USA   ISBN: 978-976-8202-81-9

NATIONAL LIBRARY OF JAMAICA CATALOGUING-IN-PUBLICATION DATA

Smith-Dennis, Colleen
    For her son / Colleen Smith-Dennis.

    p. ; cm.

ISBN 978-976-8202-81-9 (pbk)

1. Jamaican fiction
I. Title

813   dc 22

"Correct thy son, and he shall give thee rest; yea, he shall give delight unto thy soul."

Proverbs 29:17

CHAPTER 1

BJ IS BORN

Juline did not get to examine the baby when it was born because she had been in so much pain. It had been a difficult delivery, the much dreaded breech, the enemy of all pregnant mothers. The pregnancy had been going well until during the eighth month when instead of the frequent, frenzied kicking at the top of her stomach, the movements had been transferred to the middle and bottom of her uterus. A round, hard, solid mass had lodged itself at the top of her womb and refused to move. In panic she had rushed to her doctor who had informed her that somehow the baby had turned itself the wrong way and had decided to make its entry, feet first. There was little that could be done as she was almost ready for labour and because she was so vain, she opted not to have a caesarean section but a normal birth.

Well, she almost paid for this decision with her life. After the cacophony ended, and the nurse held up the child she could barely breathe. "Is it, is it alright?"

"Yes," answered the doctor, "he is alive and loud, squawking away like an angry bird. You are the problem now, not him."

Juline barely heard the last words as the pain gripped her. She was given a pain killer, and she soon drifted off to sleep, leaving the baby to his father, her mother and the medical staff.

The following day she summoned a little strength and requested that the baby be brought to her. She gazed at him as if he were the first baby she had ever seen; as if her four-year-old son had not been a baby too. To her, he was almost perfect; the complexion was just right, olive just like hers. He had a full head of hair which promised to be curly as his father's. Already the elongated face had a hint of manliness, and there were the brown eyes, not yet bright and strong, but she knew they would soon become as piercing and provocative as hers. He had his father's nose, straight except where it curved at the nostril. She would have liked it to be straighter, but at least there was the stare … his father's. Juline was pleased, almost euphoric. This was how she had wanted Jared, her first son, to look. From the outset everybody could see that he was going to be a little dark like his deceptive, devious father. Whom she claimed had tricked her into a relationship by pretending he was an affluent man but had turned out to be just ordinary and working-class.

She gazed at her baby with awe and started constructing his life: the best clothes, preparatory, not primary school, traditional high school, Ivy League university; everything that was bourgeois. She would dedicate herself to him even more than Jared because Jared was now a big boy and could take care of himself. And what would she call him? He must have his father's name, Bernard Horatio Hemmings, an old but prestigious name. Moreover, Bernard would not dare leave, because he now had a son to continue his family line. He already had three daughters and had wished over and over for a son. She could not wait to offically present the child to him! All the pain was forgotten like the wind which comes and goes. Juline kissed her baby and hugged him tightly.

ঌଌ৽৵৽৽ঌଌ৽৵৽

BJ as he was known was a bundle of noise and antics. He firmly established a place in the hearts of his over-indulgent parents and family members. Jared, his older brother, was enthralled by him and often sat beside his mother playing with him and laughing at his antics. He loved attention, and whenever he was not sleeping, his mother or the helper could be seen carrying him around, because as soon as he was placed in the crib he started howling as if he were being abused, or as if hunger or discomfort had assailed him. His mother would rush to him, pick him up and talk to him: "Hey Junior wat's wrong? Mommy just step out for a little while. You know Mommy not leaving you to go anywhere at all, Pet. You don't have to be afraid. Don't cry like that. Mommy will always be with you." She would then kiss him into giggles and then take him to his father or whoever was around to show him off.

"Just look at him smile! Have you ever seen anyone so cute before?"

"Miss Jule, yuh no memba how Jared did pretty wen him was a baby? The two of dem have the same cute smile," said Betty, the helper, who had been with the family ever since Jared was a baby. Even though she loved the new baby, there was a special spot in her heart for Jared. She thought BJ, at six months, was too spoilt and noisy. How could one baby scream so much like Jared's plugged in electronic train whistle?

"Yes, Betty, you right, but dis one just sweeter than sugar you must admit. Look at the pretty dimples just like him father! All the girls them mus' eat him up when him grow up!" she chirped, looking adoringly at BJ.

"Yes, ma'am, di two a dem. You going have hole heap a problem with di two a dem," said Betty smiling up at BJ. "Ma'am you really bless fi true, two lovely boys." Her round, eager face widened into a smile and her black seed-like eyes dilated in anticipation.

"You right, Betty, you right, but I know this one will give more problem, much more problem, you watch an' see." With that she moved out of the kitchen and walked outside into her inviting yard. The Hemmings lived in the thriving community of Heatherville, a middle and upper class community, sprawled comfortably at the base of

Carlyle Hill. These capacious or extensive houses kept their distances from one another. Intricately designed walls also assisted in this role of aloofness by keeping at bay the unwelcome, the intruders and the prying eyes. These walls also proved to be solid guards of what was desired to be kept in; the children, those who were stricken with sickness and senility, and the sordid secrets of the affluent which only the helpers whispered abroad. The houses were not mere structures but were hallmarks of architecture, designs that would make even monarchs take more than a second glance. Many of the houses boasted pools, neatly shorn lawns edged with a kaleidoscope of small flowers and healthy, playful green plants giggling in the constant wind that flowed from the hills behind the community

The houses on Carlyle Hill, spread-eagled on their hilly perches, peered down on Heatherville; their only advantage being their lofty height and the salubrious climate to which those who worked out escaped to after a hot day in the city.

It took only one look at the arrangements of the plants and gardens to tell that the Hemmings had carved their niche among the upper echelons of society. Surrounding their house were tall palms and well-dressed evergreens standing aloof while the smaller plants and radiant flowers cowered at their feet. The garden reminded one of a well laid-out dish, garnished with colourful fruits and vegetables or squares and rectangles of embroidery edged with the rainbow. There were narrow concrete walkways between each garden. The mesmerizing gardens boasted three fountains;

the most riveting was a gold and black eagle clutching its prey, a smaller bird which spurted water all over it. It was close to this fountain that Juline sat with BJ. As soon as the baby saw the bird it started babbling vigorously and pointing towards it.

"You are a very smart boy, aren't you?" she cooed adoringly. "Yes, that's the eagle, the king of all birds. It is the symbol of power. You are going to be strong and powerful just like the eagle, strong and powerful subduing all undesirables!" She looked directly into the baby's eyes as if he understood every word she spoke. He responded by laughing and babbling and pointing towards the birds.

Juline was enjoying herself, even though she felt a little tired because of BJ's demands, she felt free and unencumbered. She had given up her job as a systems manager in the large corporation where she had worked for eight years, right after leaving university. She had continued working after she had Jared at age twenty one, leaving him mostly with Betty and her mother during the days. They got married within a year and had moved right to their present house. She was trying to explain to Bernard why she had given up her job.

"But, Jule, why do you want to give up your job? Jared is now going to school and Betty is here to take care of the baby. I know you don't really have to work but..."

"Bernard, I not only have the responsibility for one child, but two children now. I need more time than just after work. You don't want you one son to get proper care?" She underlined the one son with a lowered emphatic voice and then looked at him with the piercing, provocative eyes which had drawn him to her. She knew how to use those eyes to get her own ways.

"Well, Miss, have it your way. You will soon get tired of sitting at home doing nothing," he said, emphasizing the nothing in a loud voice. He was a big man, six feet six, and endowed with bulging biceps, an attractive forty-year-old man who kept himself in good shape by exercising daily. He never failed to pull the attention of the opposite sex. Juline's mother had warned her about his age, experience and attractiveness, but her words had hit a wall and bounced off.

"Nothing! Are you referring to our son as nothing? I thought you loved your one son!" She stared at him, hurt as if he had hit her.

"Jule, you always have a way of twisting things. You know I don't mean the boy is a nobody. You know I love my son. I was just referring to giving up your demanding job and just staying home, I thought you modern women had a problem with a woman's place being in the home or is this just a whim." He looked at her as if searching for an answer to this sudden surrender of contemporary female liberty.

"Well, Bernard, this will not be forever. It will just be until BJ starts going to school. If I stay home after that then that is when I will really have nothing to do as you put it!"

"Well, Miss, suit yourself. Just remember to tell me when you are tired – tired of not dressing up and driving your SUV!" He had picked up the baby out of the crib, played with him for a while and then left for his study. He was involved in a business partnership with his father and older brother and sometimes did quite a bit of work at home. They enjoyed comfortable financial gains from importing and selling motor vehicles at two different outlets and also dabbling in horse racing.

CHAPTER 2

❧❧❧❧❧❧❧❧❧❧❧❧

VISIT TO GRANDMA'S HOUSE

One Sunday afternoon after Bernard had left for a family meeting, Juline decided to visit her parents who lived in the community of Princevale, a lower middle-class residential area. It was about three miles from where she lived. Betty had gone home for the weekend, and with Bernard gone she felt a little lonely for company other than her two children. She dressed her children carefully in expensive jeans, polo shirts and fashionable leather slippers. Her children must always look the best she decided. Moreover, she wanted her family to see how prosperous and happy she was. Her mother must recant her opinion of her marriage especially when she saw how handsome her last boy was and how well he was growing. She herself was dressed in a taupe and lavender sleeveless dress that embraced her hips and flared gently at the hem. She had matching high-heel sandals, handbag and a bandoo studded with sequins. She had put shoulder length braids in her hair although her hair was not short, but in her excuse to

9

Bernard who objected to "people's dead hair" she declared she did not have time to comb her hair every day when she had her children to attend to especially BJ, who commanded so much of her time.

She strapped her children into the back of her Honda CRV and put on the child's lock. "Jared, play with your brother if he doesn't fall asleep. I don't want him fussing too much," she commanded as she pulled out of the driveway.

It was a tranquil afternoon. The wind was resting, and the sun, seemingly tired, barely smiled. The people and the traffic, as if taking their cue from the elements, were very few, the road was almost virtually empty and in a few minutes Juline was at her parents' home. She was not the only sibling who had thought of visiting her parents; her two sisters, Angina and Kimeral, were already there sitting on the verandah talking to their parents, France and Esmine Bond. Her sisters' three children, Patrene, Levaugh and Richard, were playing with a tricycle at the front. They were taking turns pushing each other down a narrow concrete drive which led to a side gate. They all rushed to greet their aunt and cousins as soon as they got out of the vehicle. Juline hugged them and enquired about their health.

"How are you all?" Don't tell me, you are all fine. I can see that you are enjoying yourselves. Jared and BJ here are your cousins… say hello."

"Hello," Jared said willingly, but BJ clung to his mother's dress and pulled away from the children when they tried to touch him.

"He'll soon get used to you, don't mind him. Jared go and tell your grandparents and aunts hello, and then you can go and play." She placed Jared in front of her and then held BJ's hand and walked towards the verandah.

"Good evening Mummy, good evening Daddy. Gina and Kim, how you do? Glad to see everybody," she quipped.

Jared went around and greeted everyone, and they all remarked on how handsome, healthy and well-dressed he was. His grandparents made him feel especially welcome. Then it was time to greet and fuss over BJ, who had been clinging to his mother's dress all along.

"BJ, come to Grandma. You don't long to see me?" asked his grandmother.

"No," said BJ, who was almost two years old and possessed a vocabulary which consisted mainly of negative resistance words.

"Come, little man, come and sit beside di ole man nuh," invited his grandfather, creating a space for him on the seat beside him.

"No, man," said BJ and stuck out his tongue like a lizard at his grandfather, "No man, no!"

Everyone laughed except his grandparents. "Okay, Sir, since you don't like us, no drink for you!" said his grandfather.

"Mummy, dink. Want dink," BJ insisted, starting up one of his train engine wail.

"Okay son, calm down. Mummy soon get drink for you," chimed in Juline. She started towards her car, but her mother's voice halted her.

"Jule, we have plenty drink inside for the children. When you come here you don't have to bring drink." Her mother's voice had a slightly hurt tone.

"Ah know Mummy, but him so funny. Him don't drink any and everything." She continued on her way to the car amidst the questioning glances from everyone seated on the verandah. She fed BJ and then went back to the verandah, holding his hand. For a while, there was an uncomfortable silence, and then Angina started a conversation about the latest news of the day.

Sometime during the discussion, BJ wandered off and made his way to where the children were playing. For a while he just stood and watched them. They gathered around him and cajoled him into playing with them. They placed him on the tricycle and pushed him around. Juline looked up and saw him and felt pleased that he was playing with them and receiving so much attention.

Soon the children got tired of pushing BJ around and tried to pry him from the tricycle. He refused to get off and started biting at anyone who tried to get him off, screaming as he did so. Levaugh grasped him around the waist and tried to coax him, but BJ's canine tendencies surfaced and he sunk his little teeth into Levaugh's shoulder as if he were eating food, screaming as he did. The screaming of both children brought the adults running.

"My baby, my baby, what is wrong with my baby?" shouted Juline as she tried to pull the screaming BJ from Levaugh. It was quite a job as BJ seemed intent on eating Levaugh.

"What is wrong wid your baby? Don't you see that him biting Levaugh like a dog!" shouted Kimeral, Levaugh's mother. She was trying to lift up Levaugh who was writhing and screaming in pain. She, along with the help of the other adults managed to hold Levaugh, who cried even louder whenever anyone touched his bleeding shoulder.

"Okay, honey, don't scream so much, never mind," said his grandmother, trying to soothe him.

"But mi shoulder a hurt mi," sobbed Levaugh. "Him bite out mi flesh."

"Okay, let me look at it," said his mother. The words were easier said than done as more than one persons had to hold him and pull the shirt out of the bitten area. While this was being done, Levaugh screamed as if they were biting him again.

It was really a bad bite; the teeth marks had penetrated the flesh like a knife sinking into a mango, and like the juice of a ripe mango, the blood was dripping in different directions. Kimeral was really mad.

"How could a mere little pickney bite anybody like this? Tell me now, how could one little pickney do dis? She glowered at BJ as if commanding him to answer the question. BJ, now composed, looked back at her all calm and unperturbed; for him the incident was past and he was safe in his mother's arms.

Esmine Bond took charge of the situation. "We have to put disinfectant on it and take him to the doctor. It is already puffy and black. It might poison his whole body. Look how him look weak and sick." She held his hand and steered the sobbing child towards the verandah. "Kim and Gina, you better go with him."

"I'll take them, Mummy," Juline offered. "My car is faster."

"No, no I'll take him myself in my car," Kim said, without looking at her. She did not refuse the money Juline handed to her as she pulled out of the driveway.

When they had driven off, Esmine Bond asked, "What happen out there? Tell me now, what happen out there?" She looked directly at the children, willing them to answer.

"We only try to get him off the tricycle, but he wouldn't come off. Him jus' sink him teeth into Vaughn hand," Richard said in a sorrowful rush.

"But why you never come and call me since him don't want to come off? Why you never call me?" Juline interjected defensively. "Call me, that's what you should have done. And you, Jared, what you did stand up there doing when all this was happening? Tell me," she turned on Jared, who moved closer to his grandmother.

"Mummy, him would ah bite mi same way, just like him always bite me an' hit me when ah try to stop him from doing anything," Jared said plaintively. "You always say I mus' leave him alone cause him don't know what him doing."

"That don't mean you not to call me if things not going right. It don't mean that at all," she countered, glowering at Jared as if she wanted to hit him.

14

For the first time, her father spoke, "Jule, whether a child is three or ten, you have to correct dem when dem do things that not right. You must start correcting a child from him come outta the womb. You take you time, an' little by little him learn. But if you allow him to tink that because him is an infant him can do anything, that is the start of worries. Worries that will never stop here so, you mark my word." He looked at her as if she too were a child that needed counselling.

"But, Daddy, he is only a baby..."

"The child is almost two years old. More than old enough for you to correct him! 'Train up a child in the way he should go, and when he is old he will not depart from it.' That's what the blessed book say, and it is never wrong."

"Daddy, you don't know what the psychologists say about a two-year-old. They call it 'The Terrible Two' period, this is when a child likes to explore, love to have his own way and give a lot of trouble." Juline reeled off the information, glad to have psychological backing on her side.

"Listen girl," Mr. Bond said, "I have raised four children, your mother and myself, and we tried not to spoil you too much. Psychology is fine, but reality is a different game altogether. You always stubborn, but listen if you do what you mus' do no pickney can't bite off you ears!" He looked pleadingly at her, begging her to understand.

Juline was tired of that hackneyed tale, bite off ears indeed! What did they expect her to do, beat her baby when he didn't even know what he was doing? Let them stay there and bother themselves. She would tell him what to do when the time came and he was old enough to understand. Too much old-fashioned austerity would rob the child of enjoying his best days, those of childhood. They had broken in Jared, when she had lived with them, but she and her husband would raise their child instead, and he would come out just right! Didn't they see how handsome and intelligent he looked? She stood looking at her father, her thoughts churning like the mixture in a blender. Finally she said, "Well, I'm very sorry for what has happened, but it's not as if the baby did it on purpose. I'm very sorry."

In the next ten minutes she was ready to leave. She said hasty goodbyes, secured her children in the car, left an uneasy atmosphere behind and escaped to her sanctuary, her home.

CHAPTER 3

AT HOME

BJ was asleep by the time they got home. Juline tenderly put him to bed, dreaming his dreams for him as she watched him sleep. She fell more in love with him each time she watched him sleep. It wasn't that she did not love Jared, but BJ somehow seemed more adorable. As the thought of Jared came to mind, she remembered that she had to talk to him seriously. She decided to talk to him downstairs because she did not want to wake up BJ. For the time being, she allowed them to share one room during the night because she did not want BJ to be by himself. The sleeping arrangement consisted of a single bunk bed being placed in BJ's room. It didn't occur to Juline that every time the child woke up and cried in the night; that Jared's sleep was disturbed and that he would normally lay awake for quite a while before going back to sleep. This caused him to fall asleep in his stepfather's SUV every morning and made him sleepy during his morning classes.

Jared had somehow sensed her mood from she was at her parents' home and had remained quiet all the way home. He had gone to sit quietly by himself instead of following her up to BJ's room.

"Come here, Jared!" she ordered sternly as soon as she entered the room and sat down forcefully in the loveseat, causing it to protest loudly.

Jared got up with much diffidence and walked unsteadily and stood before her, "Yes, Mummy." The last word tapered off into an indistinct sound.

"Why did you have to go and tell everyone about BJ biting you and what I said to you? Who told you to tell everybody that?" As she spoke she became incensed, and without warning she grabbed Jared's shirt front and hit him, once, twice on his arm. "Next time don't go and tell your grandparents about anything at all that happens in this house, you hear me!" She shook him and then let him go suddenly, causing him to fall backwards.

As if realizing how harsh she had been, she jumped up and helped him up. "I didn't mean for you to fall, but you need to keep your big mouth zipped. You understand me?" She helped him back to his seat and then ordered him to go and brush his teeth and get ready for bed.

Jared, too shocked to cry or ask a question as he would normally do, looked at his mother as if she had landed from another world, disbelief etched in his face.

After he was gone, Juline sat for a while as if disoriented. She could not understand her behaviour; everything had happened so fast, the earlier events and then this episode with Jared. Was she over-reacting? Had Jared spoken as a child just like BJ had acted as a baby? She was not sure anymore, she felt confused and wished her husband would come home. At least he loved his baby boy and would support her. Her family had not seemed to be all that taken with BJ especially after he had bitten Levaugh. Well she didn't have to go to see them too often, just often enough for them not to think she had deserted them or was acting snobbishly.

The next morning at breakfast Jared was so quiet that his stepfather could not help noticing it. As stepfathers go, he was a good person. He did not seem to be affected by the fact that Jared was not his real child. He normally included him when he was playing with BJ and would bring him little presents occasionally. That morning he looked at the boy and asked, "Jared, you feeling sick or you don't want to go to school, which one?"

Jared looked up at him with tears in his eyes, but did not answer. Instead, he lowered his eyes and paid rapt attention to his porridge as if it were the singular most important thing in the world.

"Hey, Jared, what's up? Jule, what wrong with Jared this morning?" He threw the question at Juline, sure to get an answer.

Juline cleared her throat and recounted the previous afternoon's incident, giving her own slant to the story. She omitted the fact that she had slapped Jared and that he had fallen.

"But why didn't you tell me about this from las' night?" asked Bernard agitatedly.

"You came in late and went straight to bed and I didn't want to bother you." Juline excused herself quickly.

"Dear God, I certainly hope that the child is not too hurt to go to school or not in too much pain. You had better call and find out or go and see him today. Make sure he is all right and give your sister enough money to cover the cost. But tell me why BJ bite up the little boy like that? Ah still don't understand it at all!" There was consternation on Bernard's face as he asked the question.

"As I tell you, they were trying to drag him off the tricycle, instead of calling me to take him off," Juline replied defending BJ.

"But why they need to call you? It's not all the time that children call big people for things like that. And even if you are family, people don't take kindly to anyone biting up their children. I certainly would be mad if anyone bite up my girls or Jared or BJ like that."

"But Bern, BJ is only a baby and him not really responsible for all that…"

"Yes, he is little more than a baby, but you think anybody going to look at that when their children are in pain. Remember that him soon start school, and I don't want any problem with him and people pickney so you better try get it out of him!"

Juline was aghast. She had not expected Bernard to take that stance. He seemed to be taking sides with the others instead of his own son. Well, this was really unexpected. "So what you expect me to do?" she asked, pouting petulantly. "What I must do?"

"Well, Jule, you are his mother. You stop working to grow him up, so please do that." He looked at her, his gaze unwavering and no-nonsense. "And by the way, ah still don't hear what is wrong with Jared. Why him look like a bird that lose its wings?"

This time it was Jared who spoke, "Mummy beat mi because mi sey BJ always biting." He kept his head and eyes lowered, not daring to look at his mother.

"Well, Jared is your child and ah suppose you free to beat him when you want to, but if he is telling the truth bout BJ, ah don't see why you have to beat him." He had a strange look on his face and looked from one to the other. As if to salvage the situation, he said, "Come Jared, brush your teeth and come. Time for school."

Jared rose quickly, glad to be released from the tense situation. He did as he was told, bid his mother goodbye and fled behind his stepfather. He did not want to think about coming home after school.

CHAPTER 4

BJ GOES TO SCHOOL

There was much excitement in the Hemmings' household. It was the first Monday in September and BJ was ready for school. Just like his first attempt to sit up, creep, his first step, his first tooth and his birthday parties, his first day at school was fixed on photographs. It was not clear who was more excited, BJ, Jared or his parents. He was photographed by himself as well as with his whole family.

When they were ready for school he wanted to take some of his toys with him. When he was told that he could not, he started screaming like a fire engine hurrying to a fire. He would have thrown himself to the ground, but his father grabbed him and told him he was not going to school anymore as the teacher would not allow cry babies into the classroom. Bernard had pretended to start removing his uniform and that stopped him from screaming.

When they arrived at the Heatherville Preparatory School, the place was swarmed with children and parents from affluent communities in the country. The breeding, language, dress and the type of motor vehicles all spoke of prosperity and comfort. It was an exclusive school, and most of the parents had registered their children when they were only a few months old. Those who had not registered their children, used their influence, positions and money to gain a place.

Juline felt as if she had arrived. These were exactly the type of children that she wanted her child to mix with; the rich and the famous, the intelligent and the influential. Jared was going to a preparatory school nearby; it was good, but not as prestigious as this one. He was doing alright and had only two years left there so she would not bother to move him. She beamed at all the parents and spoke warmly to all the teachers. She kept close to her husband, who had accompanied her, hoping that everyone would notice what a handsome couple they were. She kept looking at him, and every time she got the opportunity she introduced him as her husband.

After the principal's welcome speech, she followed BJ to his classroom and placed him in the front row. "Sit right here so that you can hear everything that the teacher says;" she instructed gently. She helped him to arrange his school bag underneath his desk and his lunch bag on the neat, clean shelves provided. She then kissed him goodbye, expecting him to start bawling like so many of the children in kindergarten were doing. For some reason he did not rush to hide his face in her dress or cry until she picked him up. He sat at his desk and smiled and waved at both parents until they disappeared. When his mother crept back to see if he was really being a big boy, he was still sitting, staring outside with a vacant look on his face.

As soon as Juline had left, BJ took up his bag and installed himself at the back close to a window, where he could see what was happening outside. The teacher saw him and called him back to the front. He looked at her annoyingly for a moment, and then he went back but as soon as she turned her back to speak to a parent, he re-installed himself in his former position. A little girl took the opportunity to sit at the vacant front seat. When the teacher turned around and saw that he had gone back, she fixed him a stern stare, then looked at the little girl who had taken possession of the vacant seat. She shrugged her shoulders and decided to leave him there. "He must be one of the spoilt ones we get every year. He's obviously used to having his own way. Let him stay there," she remarked to herself, going over to talk to another parent.

BJ's first week was basically uneventful, he did whatever he was assigned very quickly and spent the rest of his time doodling. As soon as his motor skills had started developing and he could hold a pencil he had displayed an aptitude for art. He would draw some of the little things that caught his attention such as the gardener's shears, cutlery, utensils and his toys. As soon as he had completed his work at school he would take out his sketch pad and doodle away. His mother had proudly furnished him with the material for art, and she had boasted to her friends and family that BJ was a prodigy in his own right. She also remembered to mention that nine-year-old Jared also did exceptionally well at piano and guitar, talents he had acquired from his father's side of the family.

After one year at school it was clear that BJ was an intelligent child. Without much effort, he was at the top of the class, and the teacher often showed off his work to the other teachers. No one was as delighted as his parents, especially his mother. Every opportunity that she got, she would exhibit his work and she would reward him with more and more toys.

After observing the toys that BJ never played with Betty remarked one day:

"Miss Jule, you need to get one room alone for BJ toys, they get too much and they all over the place. Him not even playing wid half a dem."

"Well, Betty, now that I plan to let him sleep on his own, you can move out the bunk bed and I'm going to get a whole set of shelves so that he can get more space. He should have all his toys at his disposal when he is ready for them."

That was exactly what she did, and soon BJ got new bedroom furniture and more space for his toys. Betty noticed that this special favour was not extended to Jared. It was not that he was not given any new things, but they were given at a much slower pace and with less exuberance. Betty, in trying to rationalize the two different attitudes of the same mother to her two sons, concluded that Mr. Bernard was not Jared's father and so it was natural that more of his money would be spent on his son. This didn't seem to be a good conclusion, she decided later, because Mr. Bernard treated the two boys with fairness. She often watched him with the two boys, and he did not seem to favour one over the other. She thought it strange that it was the mother, who should be impartial, who was showing the partiality. At breakfast and at dinner she would give BJ whatever he asked for. It was a joke to her when BJ pushed his hands into Jared's food and took what he wanted. When Jared objected, she told him that there was more to be had so he didn't need to object so much. When BJ drew things on Jared's assignment, it was his genius that was praised and not the fact that Jared would have to do over his assignment. Jared often suffered silently and complained only to Betty and his grandparents because his mother would almost always find a way to excuse BJ. Betty knew where this would lead, enmity between siblings, but she dared not give her opinion because she needed her job and moreover she didn't have any education so she couldn't advice the educated. One of these days when BJ whacked Jared with one of his toys, she was certain that Jared would react in a negative manner, which would cause problems in the house.

BJ's kindergarten years into grade three were characterized by a series of quiet periods and misdeeds. His mood swings kept the teachers on edge, the children in anger and awe and his parents in agitated expectancy, waiting to be summoned when the next misdeed was committed. There was the time, in his second year in kindergarten, when he displayed his skills in pyrotechnics during the recess period. He had somehow acquired a lighter and first lit his bag of books, then the boys who sat on either side of him. When he got to the fourth one, one of the older students passed by and shouted, "Fire! Fire! K2 is on fire!"

Footsteps stampeded to the classroom, shouts reverberated all around, as those within earshot pounded towards the classroom as if they were being hounded by the fire and not going towards it. They pushed themselves into the classroom and watched in silence as if observing a minute for the dead, three small furious fires bobbing and weaving in coloured frenzy towards the ceiling. The grey smoke not to be outdone, curled itself into the flames keeping the grandeur for a while, before it too reached for the ceiling. Released from shock, two teachers grabbed the fire extinguisher and tried to put out the fire assisted by two of the groundsmen who had come running at the shouts of fire.

When BJ's parents arrived, they were visibly shaken by the sight of the partially charred desk top and the very subdued child, who sat in the principal's office as if nothing unusual had transpired. His mother rushed to hug him while his father flashed fury at him. Bernard was quiet all the way home. As soon as he alighted from his SUV, he yanked open BJ's door and dragged him screaming into the house. Betty rushed out of the house when she heard the screaming.

"Wat wrong with BJ… is he in pain?"

"Not now," Bernard answered quietly, "but he will be when I am finished with him."

"But, Bernard, this is not how you should deal with the problem," Juline protested, holding on to her husband's arms. "Let me talk to him and find out who set him up to do it," she implored.

For her pains, she was pushed aside roughly. He then proceeded to shower him with slaps on his posterior, hands and feet. His mother joined in the howling, but dared not interfere again. When Bernard was finished, he stomped out of the house angrily without saying a word or even looking back. While Betty discretely withdrew herself to the kitchen, Juline tried to console BJ who was screaming and kicking on the floor as if he was having an attack of epilepsy.

Then there was the incident in Grade One, when BJ, carrying out a dare, went into the females' bathroom and sat down on a chair inside as if he were a part of the bathroom fixture. There was no one inside when he went in at first, and so he made himself comfortable. His aides who were watching and waiting outside hung back in awe and anxiety to see how the first girl to enter the bathroom would react or to see what would transpire if a teacher caught him.

They did not have long to wait, a group of middle graders thronged into the bathroom, chattering noisily like birds without a care. They did not see him at first and continued their conversation unabated.

"My God, did you see that awful shirt that Sir has on?" enquired one girl.

"Good God, it looks like his wife's blouse!" supplied another.

"If my father ever wear anything looking like that it would be a big disgrace to the family! I know my mother would simply faint! He looks like the peasant farmer in our Social Studies book. Doesn't he get enough money even to dress properly?" the last girl criticized.

"I don't think it's that," said the second girl, "he just has a weird taste in clothes. Do you remember when he wore the striped burgundy pants with the yellow floral shirt? Every …" She did not finish, it was at this point that she saw BJ and screamed.

"What is wrong?" enquired the first girl, running to the door and grasping the lock in trepidation.

"Look, look over the corner, close to the shower… there's a boy in the bathroom!" she screamed again.

The other two girls followed her finger, saw BJ and screamed. All three rushed out of the bathroom screaming as if they were trying to set the world record for the loudest and most piercing scream. Everyone within the sound of their voices came running. One girl tripped and her glasses went flying from her face and urgent feet stamped them into the ground.

BJ tried to blend in with the crowd but as a result of his fire escapade, he was well known and the girls later pointed him out to the principal who called his mother. The first thing she asked was, "Did you call his father?"

"No," said the principal, "I thought that I would call you first."

"Well please do not call him; he is very busy at this time. I will deal with it," she said in a near pleading voice. "I am coming right away."

When she got to the school the first thing she did was to hug BJ. The principal noted this and thought, "One would have thought that she would have been angry at him or even give him an ugly look but, instead, it is *hug me tenderly*."

Throughout the discussion, she also noted that BJ's mother seemed not to be apologizing for his behaviour but sought to explain it away, as a dare that little boys felt they had to honour in order not to lose their standing with their friends.

"I'm not saying it is right, Mrs. Peart, but you must admit that little boys are curious and also eager not to seem to be cowards to their friends. Of his own accord he would never have gone inside the bathroom. It is just because of his friends," she said, trying to make her case.

"While I agree that boys will do certain things which are wrong because of peer pressure, I always maintain that everyone must have a mind of his or her own. This is the right time for children to be trained properly, and they must make a distinction between good and bad. They must learn that dares always involve something out of the ordinary, or else why would they be called dares? You have to teach him at home to make the right decisions." She hammered '*home*' and her shrewd eyes searched Juline's face for signs of comprehension and concurrence.

Juline could feel her temper starting to seethe; she fixed Mrs. Peart a piercing look and asked, "Are you suggesting that something is wrong at my home and that I am not raising my boy in the right way?"

"Miss, I am not insinuating anything of the sort. I am simply pointing out the role of the home. It is the first training ground. Moreover you need to face the fact that Bernard Junior is far too eccentric. This is not the first time that he has got himself into trouble. I am watching him, really watching him. Childish pranks yes or no, he has to be reined in," she said fervently and with finality.

Juline looked at her and thought, "So she is one of them who is against my son! They all seem to think that except for his natural brain he is a fiend! Well I know he isn't!"

On the way home she told BJ that if he did what his friends told him again; they would send him away from the school and he would have to go to some unimportant school that would not be as good as his present school. She conveniently forgot to tell her husband about the incident. She did not want her child's youthful enthusiasm to be wrongly interpreted. She remembered her own youthful days; she had played some pranks which had not been considered acceptable by her parents. She had been punished and had thought it quite unfair. She had vowed never to treat her children in the same way. Children needed room to express their creativity and fantasies and as long as no one really got hurt it shouldn't really be a problem. Her parents for instance were too strict. Every time she took BJ to visit she felt uncomfortable because she had to watch him carefully because her parents, especially her mother, was always correcting and chastising him for behaving like a child. The biting incident had left an acrid taste in their mouth, and they seemed to have earmarked him as a source of trouble. They were always guiding the other children away from him as if he were going to attack them. The children in turn kept him at arms length, especially Vaughn, who refused to play with BJ. If he saw BJ approaching while he was playing, he would stop immediately and go elsewhere, causing the other children to abandon their game.

BJ had taken a dislike to visiting his grandparents; in fact, he developed a Sunday afternoon phobia. Whenever he knew his mother was going to visit his grandparents, he would hide or pretend to have an ailment which would assail him an hour or so before her departure. This resulted in him being left behind if his father was at home, or Juline would postpone the visit, calling to report to her parents that BJ was ill. Juline had started visiting them at odd times during the week when she did not have to contend with BJ.

One day when BJ was eight, he came home all excited. "Mummy… mummy can I have a pool, can I have a pool? Everybody at school has a pool, and I need to learn how to swim now. I want to learn to swim like all my friends!" His eyes were alight with expectancy.

"BJ, that's a good idea, but your father would have to decide if that can happen. When him come home we will ask him, but remember, if you don't behave good when he is here, he will say no," she cautioned.

BJ was on his best behaviour for the rest of the afternoon and when his father came home, he was the epitome of good manners and behaviour. He took out all the good work he had been doing at school and showed him even though he had seen most of them already. As usual, he was impressed and praised BJ's efforts. When BJ broached the subject, he was not averse to the idea. As a matter of fact, he told him he had expressed an idea he had been playing with for a while in words. Everyone, including Jared, was elated as this would provide more pleasurable activities outdoors. Jared hoped that BJ would not declare a monopoly on the pool as he had been steadily doing with almost everything around the house. He would not allow the idea to daunt his interest and joy. Bernard told Juline that a number of the trees and the garden would have to be sacrificed in order for the pool to be a reality. She agreed readily, because a pool showed upward mobility, it was walking on par with the Jones'. What were a few plants and gardens compared to a pool? To say she was elated was an understatement. BJ could now stand on the same shoulder level with his friends at school.

By the next three weeks, the Hemmings' home was a market of activity; workmen moved too and fro purposefully trying to comply with the deadline given by the chief contractor. Jared watched from a short distance, trying not to get in the way, but BJ always had to be told to get out of the way. Some of the workmen viewed him simply as a curious little child wanting to get information on everything, while some saw him as a nuisance, always getting in the way and exhibiting a negative attitude whenever he was spoken to. On several occasions they had to call his mother to get him out of the way. Her response most of the time was, "That's how small children are, always getting into the middle of things, wanting to know how everything works. Come BJ, allow the workmen to finish their work so you can get to swim quickly." She would look at the workmen in a patronizing manner which was not lost on them.

When the pool was finished, BJ boasted about it to everyone at school who would listen to him. He invited his friends over on weekends, and his mother had to spend most of her time supervising them. She enjoyed watching the swimming activity, especially when BJ dominated or ordered everyone around. She exulted in what she saw as his natural leadership qualities and his charisma. He was a magnet that yanked everyone to him. She started imagining him grown up and being an important man in the society; everyone would know him, or know about him, as he wielded his intelligence and power. Yes, he would definitely make the news, no doubt about it!

CHAPTER 5

THE NEIGHBOUR'S DOG

The people living on either side of the Hemmings were early middle age people and elderly couples. One elderly couple, Mr. and Mrs. Marks, had come to live in Jamaica after residing in England for thirty five years. They had left Jamaica in the sixties at the height of the mass exodus of West Indians to Britain. They had made much of Her Majesty's benevolence and had endured sun, snow and snobbery and had acquired a comfortable home for themselves. Their three children had all opted to remain abroad; one had remained in England, one had migrated to Canada and the other to the United States of America. The couple's children, not forgetting their parents' struggles and sacrifices to maintain and educate them, expressed their love and gratitude by supporting them financially and visiting once or twice every year, taking along with them their children. The house came alive whenever the children visited, the sober quietness was transformed to gaiety as the children feeling a sense of freedom played outdoors, riding their bicycle, chasing one another and just laughing and having fun for the sheer pleasure of it.

The Marks had two prized dogs; one was a golden retriever and the other an American Cocker Spaniel. These two dogs even though they were reasonably good watchdogs were very friendly and made great family pets. Mrs. Marks constantly brushed the fine, silky coat of the cocker spaniel, Molly, and the often wet golden coat of the golden retriever, Sam. Sam always went wherever there was water, as his particular breed was known for swimming through icy water to retrieve birds from a river or lake. The cocker spaniel was much cockier and was more interested in romping and keeping his well-groomed coat dry.

Everyone who passed by the Marks' house and saw the dogs admired them. When their grandchildren came to visit they spent a great deal of time petting and feeding the dogs. Back home there was not much space for raising animals and running wild, so they enjoyed themselves immensely.

One summer when BJ was ten years old, all six of the Marks' grandchildren came to visit. The house was alive with the sounds of laughter and shouts. The children played outdoors with the dogs most of the time throwing sticks and other objects and getting the golden retriever to retrieve them and bring them back to them. BJ watched them as they played; at first he was amused at their simple fun, but after a while wondered how anyone could continue with the same boring activity for so long. He himself was busy practising darts and shooting his arrows into a board with different holes. He increased his distance from his target each time he aimed at them. Sometimes Jared played with him, but being a teenager now, his interests were mainly the computer, playing his musical instruments and his new hobby, writing poems. Much to his mother's disappointment, Jared had very little time for BJ. Sometimes it wasn't that he didn't have time, but he resented the manner in which BJ spoke to him and tried to order him around. When he tried to instruct him, he refused to follow what he was told, telling his brother that was not how things were to be done or that he knew already. At sixteen, Jared found this annoying, he was awaiting his Caribbean Secondary Examination (CSEC) results and considered himself too old to be taking instructions from a mere boy, so Jared often played alone or with his two best friends whenever he could get them to come to his house.

One day when BJ was shooting arrows, he became distracted by a fire engine winging and screaming its way to a fire. He missed his target, and the arrow sped over the fence into the Marks' yard. It missed Eloise, the eldest of the six children by a few inches and buried itself in the bark of an evergreen tree nearby. Eloise screamed as the arrow whizzed past her and the dogs hearing her scream started to bark and jump over the yard fiercely. The other children, on hearing her scream, ran to her side, questioning and consoling. The adults in the house also ran outside to investigate.

When they saw the arrow embedded in the tree they gasped, and after ensuring that the children had not been harmed, they tried to identify the source of the arrow.

"Where did it come from?" enquired Mr. Marks. "Did any of you see it coming?" He searched their faces, carefully hoping to receive a positive response.

"No, Grandpa, I did not see it. I just felt something fly by me, and when I looked up I saw the arrow in the tree," volunteered Eloise in a quivering voice, still visibly shaking.

Her mother moved to her side and put her arm around her. She then spoke in a voice which struggled to be calm while her black ackee-seed eyes looked enquiring at her.

"Where were you standing, Lois?" she questioned.

"I was standing beside the mango tree, playing with Sam," the child answered. "We ..."

"Margaret," Mr. Marks interrupted his daughter while studying the arrow carefully, "based on the direction in which it is pointed it came straight from across the neighbour on my right; that's the Hemmings."

"Are you sure, Grandpa?" questioned John-Mark, another of the grandchildren. He was amazed at his grandfather's quick decision.

"An arrow travels in a straight line, so based on the direction it is pointing it definitely came from the Hemmings' yard. The question is, who shot it?" He looked across at the Hemmings' property as if expecting the answer to jump out at him immediately. Getting none, he went back to the tree and wrested the arrow from it. It fell to the ground, and Sam, the golden retriever picked it up and ran off with it. He sat with it as if he were guarding it. He snarled ferociously at anyone who went close to him or who attempted to touch the arrow. While the family was trying to determine why Sam was behaving in that manner, they heard a child's voice shouting across the fence.

"Mr. Marks, Mr. Marks can you come here?"

They looked up to see a tall, sturdy boy with fair complexion and curly hair peeping through a gap in the fence. Mr. Marks did not like the sound of the voice. He did not say please or greeted them in any way, and his request closely resembled a command. As if he had summoned the whole family, everyone went towards him. They stopped a few feet from him and looked intently at him.

"Good day to you too," said Mr. Marks in a voice that suggested, you did not wish me a good day so I am doing it to you.

All this was lost on BJ as he did not return the greeting. He fired back instead, "I think my arrow came over there. Did you see it? Can you pass it for me? I need it to continue my practising." He said all of this quickly as if he were indeed in a great hurry and had no time to waste.

Instead of honouring his command, Mr. Marks asked, "What do you mean by shooting arrows carelessly around this place? You could have injured my grand-daughter with it! Do your parents know that you are shooting arrows around here? Whether they are real arrows or not, they are dangerous!" He looked fiercely at BJ, demanding answers.

"Oh, please. I was not shooting at anyone and more-over there's plenty of space around here for that. Could I get back my arrow?"

At this point Sam let out a loud growl which caused everyone to jump. He rushed at the fence towards BJ as if he had a personal argument to settle. The arrow fell from his mouth as he did so but before anyone could pick it up, he rushed back, picked it up with his mouth and rushed back to the fence, growling, baring his teeth and wagging his tail furiously like a fan turned on at the highest level. Attempts were made to quieten him and retrieve the arrow, but the friendly, family dog had become a menacing fury. It was as if he was the one whom the arrow had almost hit. His behaviour was bizarre, since he had often gone through the hole in the fence into the Hemmings' yard to visit their poodle and the half Alsatian who was only freed during the night. BJ walked away from the fence with a pensive look on his face; so they were giving him an attitude and that golden beast thought he could hold on to his arrow, well let them be, they would see.

That evening Mr. Marks watched for Mr. Hemmings when he was coming from work. Mr. Hemmings was surprised to see the elderly gentleman approach him as he turned into his gate. The Marks seldom left their house except to go to church or an occasional important business trip. He had never seen any of them on the road so he was very surprised.

"Mr. Marks, good evening. I have not seen you in a while," Mr. Hemmings said getting out of his SUV.

"Good evening Mr. Hemmings. How are you?" replied Mr. Marks, approaching Bernard. It was not the first time that he was noticing what a fine tall man Mr. Hemmings was. It was a pity that the little boy who resembled him so much, did not seem to have much manners.

"I am fine, Mr. Hemmings. I just want to bring a little matter to your notice."

Bernard wondered what it could be; but it had to be important since Mr. Marks had left his house to come and see him, "Would you care to come inside?" he asked, motioning to the gate.

"No Sir, this will not take long, only a few minutes," said Mr. Marks. He then proceeded to tell Mr. Hemmings about the incident highlighting the dangers of shooting arrows in an area occupied by humans, and BJ's impolite attitude.

Mr. Hemmings stood with his mouth slightly opened and his eyes opened even wider as he listened to Mr. Marks. He did not interrupt him but listened to the elderly gentleman. He had had no idea what Mr. Marks wanted to see him about, but this had come as an astounding revelation. When Mr. Marks had finished his complaint he said: "I thank you for telling me Sir. I am very sorry about what happened, but I am more troubled than anything else about the fact that your grand-daughter could have been injured. Please apologize to your wife, your daughter and your grand- daughter for me. Sir, you really have to step inside because that boy of mine will have to apologize to you, oh yes he will!"

He left the van where it was parked and went through the gate bellowing for BJ as he did so. Both BJ and his mother came running.

"For goodness sake Bernard, why are you shouting so much? All the neighbours in the community must be wondering what is happening here!" remarked Juline as she hurried to her husband's side. "What is happening Bernard? What …" She stopped her question as she noticed Mr. Marks standing by quietly . "Mr. Marks it is you! I have not seen you for a long time now. Is everything okay at home?" she questioned, showing real concern.

Before he could answer Bernard chipped in, "Things at his home would have been better if BJ here had behaved himself better," he fired, glaring at BJ.

"But Daddy, I didn't do nothing! It was just an accident," BJ defended himself, turning to his mother for support.

"What is this all about Bernie? What are you all accusing BJ of?" She turned to her husband for an explanation.

Bernard recounted the incident with Mr. Marks adding flesh to the skeletal details, because as usual, Bernard was not a man of unnecessary words. If something could be said in two or three sentences, then he would not use four.

When they were finished, Juline remarked, "I am sorry, Mr. Marks, but as you can see BJ meant no harm. Did you BJ? He was only having fun. I am sorry, Sir." She defended BJ.

"That is one thing, but what about him speaking impolitely to Mr. Marks? Apologize immediately and get inside until

I come," he ordered, looking threateningly at BJ. If looks could kill, BJ would have certainly dropped dead.

"I am sorry," said BJ noncommitedly without looking at Mr. Marks.

"Sorry who?" thundered his father, advancing towards him and looking askance at him.

"I am sorry, Mr. Marks," recited BJ in the same nonchalant tone.

"You can go inside now," said his father, not really satisfied but leaving it at that.

BJ looked first at Mr. Marks and then at his father before he moved off. It was not clear what the look meant but it was clearly hostile.

Later when Mr. Marks had left and Bernard went into the house, Juline asked, "Bernie why you always so harsh with BJ. He is only a child."

"Woman, you have been saying that ever since he was born. I suppose when he is one hundred you will still call him a child and defend him in everything." He looked at her briefly and then called BJ. While he was coming he added, "Somebody around here has to teach this boy that he can't always have his own way. Since I am his father and he's the only son I have, I am going to try." He countered Juline's rising protest by addressing BJ who had now arrived. "Go and get all the arrows you have inside," he instructed," and mind you bring every single one of them! You know the rules; you use the arrows only when we go to the firing range. Suppose you had hurt that girl? Do you know the trouble we would be in tonight? Tell me. You will not go back to the range for the next three months and darts will be the only thing that you practise around here. Is that clear?"

"Yes, Sir," BJ answered, anger and disbelief evident in his eyes.

When he was gone Juline tried to saddle Jared with some of the blame. She called Jared to her and asked, "Why didn't you stop BJ from playing with his arrows? You are the older one and when I am not here you are responsible for him." She looked at him accusingly, trying to make him feel guilty, but Jared had an answer ready.

"Mummy, since when does BJ listen to me? Not even when you are around BJ don't listen me. It's only when Dad is around." Jared declared, looking at his mother intently.

"Boy, what you saying to me? You trying to tell me that BJ does not listen to me either?" She was angry, boiling angry. Maybe if her husband was not there she would have struck Jared.

"Mummy, every time BJ get into trouble when I am around you always try to blame me, when you know that BJ is rude and always want to fight me. And if he licks me I am going to lick him back. I am not taking anymore lick from him or blame for what he does." He was almost close to tears. "Many times in here I get punishment for things him do wrong. I am his scapegoat. I am tired of it!"

Juline and Bernard were aghast, never had Jared spoken like this before. To Bernard, this was a release of bitterness and anger, long festering, now an open wound. He had suspected for some time that the boy was not happy, but had said nothing, not wanting to come between Juline and her son. He had noticed how withdrawn and introverted Jared had become, preferring to study in his bedroom rather than in the family room; digging into his music and poetry rather than going out with them as a family. He had not been unkind to BJ but it was not the warm brotherly relationship that true brothers had. Much of what he said was true, but he had no idea that Jared would have spoken so frankly.

For Juline, Jared had passed his boundary as a child. How dare he point an accusing finger at how she dealt with BJ? Everyone seemed to think she was spoiling BJ when she was only allowing him to express himself. And look at Jared! Look at what she had done for him? She had found a good rich man to take the place of his 'poor thing' father. Look where he was living and the lifestyle he enjoyed! If it weren't for her, he would just be an ordinary person. She was so choked with anger that she did not answer him. Bernard just sat there regarding them both; he looked from one to the other without commenting. Juline dismissed Jared in a huff and it was only after that, that he got up and went to bed, leaving the arrows on the coffee table.

Juline did not follow her husband to bed; instead, she went to console BJ. When she got to his room it was as if a cyclone had struck. Clothes, books, toys and other objects were strewn all over the room. BJ in his anger had flung all those items against the wall and on the floor. He was lying on his bed, clutching his favourite drawing book which he allowed no one to see. She sat on the bed and spoke to him in soft tones. After a while he got up and they both tidied the room as she did not want her husband or Betty to see it.

At two o'clock she went to the bathroom. She had been awakened by loud barking from the dogs and wondered what they were up to. They seemed extremely agitated, but that was how they behaved sometimes. Maybe a stray dog had wandered onto their property.

Before she went back to bed she looked in on BJ, but he was not in his room. She knocked on his bathroom door but got no response. She called him softly, still no response. She wondered if he had become hungry and had gone downstairs for a late snack so she started down the stairs. Halfway down she heard as if a door had opened and closed, and she was about to panic when BJ emerged at the foot of the stairs. They were both surprised to see each other. BJ explained that he had awoke and felt hungry and so had gone downstairs for a snack. His mother sent him to brush his teeth and went back to her bed.

He went into the bathroom, plucked some weeds from his sweat bottom, washed his slippers and then went to bed with a satisfying smile on his face.

The next day was Sunday so the whole family slept late. They only went to church occasionally, and BJ always complained for the duration of the service about being bored and wanting to go home, so Juline only went at Christmas,

New Year's Eve, Good Friday, Easter Sunday and before or after Independence.

The urgent shrilling of the telephone woke up Bernard. It was Mr. Marks and he seemed hysterical, wanting to find out if he or his family had seen his golden retriever, Sam. Bernard told him he was still in bed and he apologized and hung up.

Later when Bernard got up, he checked with Mr. Marks. He told Bernard he could not find Sam anywhere at all. He viewed this as being serious because it was the first time that had happened. Bernard joined in the search, but it was fruitless. Sam was never seen again. The Marks were devastated.

Later that day, Bernard noticed the arrows on the coffee table. He had forgotten to take them up. He was almost certain that there had been three of them. Mr. Marks had given him one and BJ had given him the other two. He must be getting senile he reflected as he took up the two arrows and went to put them away.

CHAPTER 6

BJ'S SISTERS COME TO VISIT

That same summer, BJ's sisters, Bernard's three daughters from previous relationships, came to spend the summer. The first girl, Tara-Ann, was the same age as Jared; the second, Meisha, was fourteen and the youngest, Kai, was twelve. They all had different mothers and came from different parts of the country: Tara-Ann was from St. Elizabeth; Meisha, from Clarendon; and Kai from St. Andrew. Only Meisha bore any resemblance to her father. She was slightly brown with curly hair, long face and straight nose flared at the nostrils; the others obviously took after their mothers. Tara-Ann was tall and dark with an oval face and deep, dark-brown eyes. She was generously proportioned and reminded one of a stately African princess. Kai obviously had Chinese ancestry; she was fair with a round face, small seed-like eyes and long, straight black hair.

At first Juline placed all three girls in one room, but Bernard asked why they should reinvent the middle passage when there were two other unoccupied bedrooms in the house. Juline defended her action by saying it would help to conserve electricity and the amount of bed linen to be washed. Bernard asked Juline when since had utility bills become a prime concern of hers and why couldn't the girls put their own bed linen and clothes into the washing machine and wash them themselves instead of burdening Betty.

He won the argument and Tara-Ann, the eldest, was placed into another room by herself. Juline did not like this because she was certain that in the large family that Tara-Ann was coming from she had had to share with other siblings. It was a mystery to her how Bernard had got into a relationship with anyone from such an impoverished background. She deliberately overlooked the fact that Tara-Ann exuded good breeding, a quiet sober attitude and was well-spoken. From the beginning it was obvious that her father, Bernard, was quite taken with her. He often spoke to her as if he were addressing an intelligent adult and whenever he was at home he often engaged in conversations relating to books they had both read or other topical issues. Juline's resentment of the child grew as the conversations became more and more frequent. She refused to participate as the other children sometimes did, as their father deliberately asked them questions, so that they could become a part of the discussion. She purposefully withdrew herself and went off with BJ to some other part of the house. She felt that the girl was receiving the attention that BJ should have been getting. Wasn't he the only son, the only child that was born in wedlock? Bernard was not the only one who was drawn to Tara-Ann; Jared and her two sisters often spent a lot of time with her.

On BJ's part, he saw them all as intruders. He no longer had the house and the yard mostly to himself, everywhere he went they seemed to be there. They had even invaded his favourite spot, the fountain with the yellow and black eagle. The girls often tried to include him in their activities but BJ's favourite excuse was that they were girls' games and he did not like girls' games. Tara-Ann pointed out to him that Jared was a boy and he often took part, but BJ's response was that Jared was a sissy. The only activities he wanted to participate in were swimming, dominoes and chess. Whenever he participated, he wanted to give all the orders and hog the games. For the most part, the older children went along with him and allowed him to have his own way. Sometimes they showed their resentment and refused to play the games his way.

One day tempers were ignited when they were playing dominoes, Kai said that BJ was cheating and BJ objected to being called a thief. He turned over the whole table of dominoes. As he did so, the table fell on Kai's left foot. She screamed in pain and hopped about while the others tried to console her. Without warning, she flew at BJ and hit him in his face. He looked at her in absolute disbelief, and then he hit her back in the face. Her face changed to red and immediately started swelling but she jumped at him as a feline from a tree and soon they were rolling on the ground, hitting each other. The children who were standing by debilitated by shock at the swift events, pounced on them and tried to tear them apart. This was a huge task as they were locked tightly together like carved figures.

Betty heard the noise and the screaming and ran outside. "What is happening out here?" she demanded, wiping her hands on her apron. She stopped in shock when she saw the children trying to pull apart the two on the ground. "Stop the fighting!" she shouted, but the two on the ground did not hear her. She could have been shouting from a dream or another time period for all the response she got. She continued to shout but to little avail, so she joined in trying to separate BJ and Kai, shouting at them all the time and threatening to tell their father as soon as he got in.

Finally, Betty and the other children managed to separate them. "Look at you all!" she shouted. "You getting mad or what?" What you fighting over? Is who start it?" She questioned rapidly, not waiting for an answer to one question before she went on to another. "Look at you all!" she exclaimed again.

The children were really something to behold! Their hair was dirty and filled with grass, trash and matter that they had gathered from the ground. BJ's eyes were swollen and his previously clean unmarked face now, bore a long curved gash close to his left ear. His shirt was smeared with patches of red dirt and one sleeve was almost torn off. A part of his right slipper had unglued itself. Kai looked no better. Her dress was torn at the waist and just as smeared with dirt as BJ's clothes. Her face was definitely swollen and her right eye was almost swollen shut. She was crying uncontrollably, but BJ quite calm and controlled looked at her scornfully and started flinging abuse at her.

"Why you had to come here? Why you didn't stay at your own house? This is my parents' house, not yours. All of you come here cause you want to stay in big house and eat people food, my food! You want to take over my mother's house and my swimming pool. All a you go back to you country house and stop taking up all of my space with you ugly push up self. I hate all of you!" he declared, running inside and ignoring Betty's order to get back and apologize. She might not have existed, because he didn't even look back.

Left behind, the girls looked embarrassingly at one another. BJ's words seared like soap being rubbed into the eye. They felt like nuisances. Tara-Ann had got exactly that impression from her stepmother but had tried not to let it bother her. She wondered if the others had picked it up and hoped they hadn't. She knew her father would be offended if she told him she wanted to go home so she decided against that. With Kai it was different, she wanted to go home right away.

"I am going to call my mother to come and get me," she sobbed painfully.

When Tara-Ann looked at her, her heart was pricked at her appearance. She knew that her father would be very angry if Kai called her mother without first consulting him so she advised her against it: "No Kai, let daddy deal with it when him come. That's the best thing." As an afterthought she said, "And remember that your mother is gone abroad for the holiday so you would have to stay with your grandmother and little sister." She said this triumphantly hoping to deter Kai. She went over to her and put her arms around her. Her little sister hugged her back, crying.

Betty tried to take things into control. "Come all of you... clean up youself and get something to eat. Your parents will have to deal with you wen they come home. But listen to me no more cursing and fighting or else..." she left the sentence hanging threateningly. After the girls had left to do her bidding, she tried to get BJ out of his room but he told her to go away and threw objects at the door. Feeling angry and useless, she moved away from the door. She thought of calling the parents immediately but decided against it as she didn't want to bother Mr. Hemmings, and Mrs. Hemmings would only come home and blame the girls. Jared had gone to his paternal grandparents to spend the week so he was not around. She decided to call Mr. Hemmings late in the afternoon instead.

Fate decreed that Mrs. Hemmings came in a little earlier than her husband. She thought it strange that she did not see any of the children outside or downstairs as they usually were. She called Betty and BJ at once. Betty came out of the kitchen with a look on her face which said, "I wish I was somewhere far away."

Betty, where are the children?" Juline demanded, putting her car keys away and taking off her shoes.

"Miss, dem in the room," she answered hesitantly, not divulging the story as yet.

"But that is unusual, they usually would be outside. Is somebody sick?" she enquired, looking hard at Betty and sitting down.

"Not really sick, ma'am, but they fall out today and there was a little trouble," she said unwillingly waiting for the accusation.

"Trouble? Trouble? How come there was a problem here and nobody called me to tell me about it? A hope nothing is wrong with BJ!" she got up immediately and started up the stairs shouting, "BJ, Tara, Kai, Meisha… where are you? Come to me right now!"

The girls all emerged from Tara-Ann's room and made their way downstairs. There was no sign of BJ. Juline rushed up the stairs and pounded on the door. "BJ are you okay son? Open up, come out here right now!" after a minute of constant knocking, BJ appeared, face puffed up, rag and electronic game in hand.

Juline gave a frightened scream, "My God, who did this to my child? Tell me BJ that some accident happened and that's how you hurt yourself. Don't tell me that somebody did this to you!" she shouted.

"Is Kai… she started the fight, she hit me first!" he shouted, pointing at Kai accusingly. "An' the others did not help me," he added in petulance.

Juline turned to Kai as if she were about to swoop on a lesser prey. "Who told you that you could come to this house and do this to my boy?" she questioned agitatedly. "Who told you?" it appeared as if she was going to strike her. She seemed oblivious to the fact that Kai's face was also swollen.

"Oh no you don't," said a voice from the foot of the stairs.

They all looked down and saw Mr. Hemmings. Nobody had seen or heard him come in, because of the shouting.

"Everybody go into the den right now!" he commanded. He ignored Juline's cry of, "Look what the girl did to BJ!"

When they were all in the den, Mr. Hemmings sat down, and everybody else stood, including Juline, BJ's bodyguard.

"Now I want the truth and I am going to ask everyone to tell me what happened, starting with Tara-Ann." Juline made a sound of protest but everyone ignored her. "I will punish anyone who tells a lie!" he looked at them hard without flinching.

The hearing started with the children all telling their story one by one. When they were all finished, Mr. Hemmings asked, "Why do you all say that BJ was cheating?"

"Sir, he was getting up and peeping into everybody's hand. We all saw him do it," volunteered Kai.

"But Kai, why didn't you complain to Betty instead of hitting him when he pushed over the table?" inquired Juline still trying to absolve BJ.

"He hurt me and I hurt him back, Miss!" Kai fired back.

"Sit down all of you." Mr. Hemmings ordered. He then proceeded to ascribe blame where it should be placed. Juline was quite displeased; BJ showed no emotion whatever, Kai bowed her head.

He sent the children to bathe and eat and then he told Juline severely, "Even though I married you and BJ is the only child born in wedlock, all three girls, Tara-Ann, Meisha and Kai are my daughters! They belong here just as BJ and Jared and no one is going to make them feel like intruders! I invited them here because I wanted to see all my children together. I love them all, Jared included. Do not ever speak to any of them like how I hear you talk to Kai when you didn't know I was hearing you." He was very angry and his lips trembled involuntarily.

Juline was taken aback; this could not really be her husband! This could not be Bernard, her son's father! She had no doubt that he loved BJ, but he was too harsh with him. He was always counselling, chiding, criticizing, and making everything seem like Mount Everest. What would BJ do if she were not around to console him and take his part? She noticed too that BJ was growing resentful of his father. He no longer wanted him to be involved in everything in his life, only select things, which involved money and activities for which he needed his help. She went to bed that night with that Atlas' burden in her heart. Things were certainly not going the way she had planned them.

One evening the following week, Mr. Hemmings came in from work much earlier than usual. He had a business trip to the USA the following day and wanted to get everything organized and also get a good night's sleep. He greeted the children warmly, enquired after their health and then made his way upstairs. Five minutes later he came rushing down the stairs, bellowing for all the children. "Meisha, BJ, Tara, Kai come into the den right away!" The urgency in his voice caused the girls to stop their scrabble game right away and BJ who was sitting close to the eagle playing solitaire with a pack of cards, rushed in. As they were rushing in, he called Betty. He then made a telephone call to his wife. By the time the call was finished, everyone had assembled looking perplexed, sure that something was wrong.

Mr. Hemmings scrutinized everyone as if he were seeing each for the first time, an indescribable look on his face. He spoke hesitantly, "This morning before I left home, I placed an envelope with some US dollars on a night table in my bedroom. Juline had already left for work and I am certain she did not come back here, so I am interested in finding out why it is not there now."

Everyone denied taking the money. In addition, the girls declared that they had never ever gone into their father's bedroom; they didn't know what inside his room looked like. That left two person's Betty and BJ. Betty admitted to going in there and tidying up as she did everyday, but said she had not seen an envelope much less remove one. BJ said he had not gone near the room all day.

"So you are all saying that the envelope sprouted wings and flew off somewhere. I need that money to complete some transactions tomorrow, so I need it now! I must find it! And after I finish searching around, I am going to go outside and allow you to go upstairs one by one and the person who has it just put it back in my room, I am not going to ask who it is." He looked at them pleadingly, begging them to comply.

He went back upstairs to search, but his efforts proved futile. He came back down disappointed. At this point Juline arrived home. She was both shocked and disgusted when she heard the details. Playing her usual defensive role for BJ she declared: "Well nobody has ever missed anything in this house before so this is really strange!" she allowed her eyes to rove accusingly over the girls, as her words sunk in.

"I am not accusing anyone as yet. I hope the truth will come out," Bernard said looking meaningfully at Juline.

True to his words, he called them all outside and sent them upstairs one by one. When they had all gone upstairs they went back outside to stand beside their father. It was then his turn to go upstairs to see the result. He came back downstairs almost smothered by anger. He could hardly breathe.

"Sit in the den everyone!" he managed to gasp out. I am going to search the rooms first and then anywhere else which might be a good hiding place. Juline went to help him. He insisted that they searched together. They searched

BJ's room first, and then they went into Tara-Ann's room and then the two younger girls' room.

After the search, Mr. Hemmings went into his room and threw down two envelopes on the bed. He held his head between his hands, trying not to let it explode. His brain matter was contracting and expanding violently; his heart seemed to be beating in his head and his life seemed to want to flee his weak embarrassed body. He felt faint and disoriented; maybe it would be better if his body just disintegrated. Juline stood beside him pretending to console him, but his head was bowed and he did not see the smug, snide look of triumph on her face. Her look rejoiced at the fact that she knew all along that the children were worthless and that her boy was the good one.

When Mr. Hemmings felt sanity slowly seeping back into his being, he got up and staggered silently downstairs. Juline followed him like a hound which had picked up the scent of a long sought after prey and was ready to pounce. He sent BJ and Meisha to occupy themselves elsewhere then he fixed his attention on Tara-Ann and Kai.

"Why did you do it?" he enquired calmly, his previous anger now replaced by bewilderment.

"Do what, Sir?" they chorused together looking at each other incredulously.

"You know what you did? Why did you do it? Do you think you could get away with it? Why did you do it?" he fired away, not waiting for an answer to each question.

"I do not know what you are talking about, Sir," said Tara-Ann. "I have done nothing." She looked at her father as if he had lost command of his senses.

"Didn't you steal my money and put it in your suitcase both you and Kai?" he looked straight in her eyes willing her to deny what was true.

Her eyes widened and she blinked as if she were trying .to get some foreign body out of her eyes. She looked her father straight in the eyes and mindful that she was talking to her father she said calmly, "Sir, I am not a thief. Even if you found your money in my suitcase I did not put it there. I am not a thief!" she emphasized without raising her voice.

"You have to give her credit," Mr. Hemmings thought. "Even in the thick of this disgrace she manages to be calm and sound convincing. What a girl."

Kai was crying. It seemed of late that was her favourite past time. Her crying became sobs which caused her body to shiver spontaneously. Tara-Ann moved over to her and held her against her, trying to comfort her. While all this was happening Juline sat by enjoying the kill. There was no need to say anything. Their businesses were being taken care of. She had got her desire. Now he would reinstate their son to his former position of importance and dominance. So much for their encroachment! Now they would have to go back from whence they came. She pretended to cough and covered her mouth, laughing into her hands.

Mr. Hemmings did not know why, but he knew that something was wrong. Somewhere doubt of his daughters' guilt germinated in his mind. The facts were undeniable but questions like his conscience nagged him, "What if they were speaking the truth? But who could have placed the money in their suitcases?"

CHAPTER 7

BJ IN HIGH SCHOOL

There was much celebration in the Hemmings' household; BJ had passed his Grade Six Achievement Test (GSAT) for the school of his choice. The year before Jared's success in the CXC and his entry into sixth form also generated celebration. For his efforts he was given a trip abroad. BJ's success was also celebrated by a trip to Canada and additionally a horse.

BJ had become interested in riding because Brandon, his best friend since preparatory school, had boasted to him that horseback riding was a thrill. It gave one a sense of mastery, knowing that one was in control of a huge beast once he or she acquired the skill of controlling its movement. To Brandon, it also made one seem to rise above the lowly world, stomping on, directing and suppressing things beneath. BJ liked the sound of this and had been pestering his father for a horse for the past two years. His father's reluctance was masked in the large sum he quoted for such an animal connected to the sport of kings. Juline thought that BJ deserved the horse and had contributed a portion of the money to purchase it. There was nothing too good for her son.

As soon as the result was known, BJ's wildest expectation was fulfilled. His father took him to Mr. Jemison, who lived about a mile away and had a huge property on which he bred horses and dogs. BJ was presented with a grey three-year-old thoroughbred. This kind of horse, related to the Arabian horse which can live in the dry desert was very powerful. It was only used for riding but also for racing, show-jumping and hunting. The horse stood fifteen 'hands' tall and promised to grow even taller, because it is said that horses continue to grow until they are four years old. Looking at the horse, BJ could see the awesome power exuding from its flanks. The ribs rippled slightly like those of an athlete with a powerful physique; the mane was not very long, but it looked clean and well curried like the horse's coat; the tail flared out behind it like Jecelia's hair, the Indian girl from his grade five and six classes. BJ named him Black Eagle as his promising strength reminded him of the gold eagle at home.

Mr. Hemmings told BJ that he would be able to ride on Mr. Jemison's property on weekends, where he would be supervised by Benjy, one of the stable hands. Mr. Hemmings also told him, that he would start his riding lessons on one of the ponies on the property, until he was able to manage his own horse.

BJ was ecstatic about his new toy and boasted to everyone at school about it. School became uninteresting and faded in importance when compared to riding and Black Eagle. BJ could not wait for Fridays to come to see his horse. He dreamt of the day when he would be in total control of it.

Grade seven at Spring Gardens High for BJ was dreary. His natural intelligence seemed to have suffered a blow. He paid very little interest in class and did very little work. His homework was very often undone, because when he was asked at home if he had homework, he said there was none. He failed to turn up at classes with his textbooks, even though his mother had purchased every single one of them. He was more drawn to playing pranks in class and arguing with his teachers. When he was caught throwing paper or talking out of turn, he blamed other students and engaged the teachers in fruitless arguments, aimed at diverting everyone's attention from the lessons. His friend Brandon was in the same class with him. They were as close as the dermis and epidermis.

When Juline went to collect BJ's monthly report, she just stood looking at the piece of paper in her hand, as if she could not understand the characters printed on it. She was expecting marks in the nineties that she knew BJ was capable of, but instead mere forties and fifties, except for Art, hit her eyes. She decided to speak to the teachers and during consultation she learnt of BJ's pranks and inattentiveness. She left with the promise to deal with the problems but at the same time she instructed the teachers to make their lessons more interesting so that BJ would pay more attention. She pointed out to them, that he was a very brilliant child and that something must be happening or must have happened, to prevent him from excelling as he normally did. One teacher told her that it was her duty to monitor her child and find out what was happening in his life. He alluded to the fact that something must be wrong at home because his homework was not done and he did not take his textbooks to school.

Juline, quick to point out what she thought were other people's errors but defensive whenever a finger was pointed at her, vehemently denied that anything was awry in her home. She painted a picture of close constant attention, bounteous love and impeccable moral scrutiny and upbringing. She fell short of upbraiding the teacher for such an unfounded thought and hinted that her job was to teach and not speculate on his students' private life.

She left the school with a tart taste in her mouth. "So much for their excellent record when they couldn't even grab the attention of a brilliant grade seven child!" She complained to Bernard about the teacher's insinuation.

"Can you imagine, he had the gall to tell me that something was wrong at my home why BJ was not learning!" she told Bernard when he asked to see the report.

"Why did he say that?" Bernard asked, a bit hurt by the comment.

"He said he did no homework and took no textbooks to school," she blurted out before realising that she would be damning herself.

"Juline, is it the teacher or the parents who are supposed to see that homework is done and that children take books to school?" he enquired, looking at her in a hurt manner.

"But Bernard, when I ask BJ about homework he don't have any. Can I supervise what I don't see?" she fired back. "And by the way, all three of us suppose to help him with homework!" she emphasized, averse to being blamed for everything.

"That is true, but you are normally at home before me most evenings. Do you want me to come home and pack his bag for him and help him with his homework when you are here doing nothing? Tell me so I can start from tonight, moreover why should one little boy, who just start high school neglect his homework and don't take his books to school? The teacher has a point painful as it is." He hammered home his point and not waiting for her defence he called BJ.

When he was coming she remarked, "You always want to put blame on me for everything concerning BJ. When you not blaming me, you blaming BJ!" She was really annoyed.

"If you were really fair you would see that you really spoiling the boy! Spoiling the boy and taking up for him in everything, even when him wrong," he raged, glad at the opportunity to really tell Juline his mind.

BJ came while he was making the last comment. He stood looking at his father anticipating the worst.

"What is the meaning of these grades?" his father demanded. "You better have a good explanation!" he thundered facing him fully.

"The classes are boring, and I don't understand some of the things, Sir," he answered readily as if he had prepared the answer beforehand.

"All you need to do is listen and ask questions if you don't understand." His father instructed. He then added, "But boy, if you can't understand simple grade seven work at the beginning of the term, how the hell you going to manage for five years? You tell me that."

"But, Sir, some of the teachers not nice and they don't always want you to ask questions," he said sounding really earnest. "Especially Mr. Sanders, him really don't like me," he added, trying to strengthen his case and gain his father's sympathy.

He realized he had lost when his father countered, "You go to school to learn not to like anybody special! And if I ever see grades like these in this house again you will see!" With that he dismissed him. BJ looked at him in a peculiar way which caused Bernard's heart to freeze. He felt suddenly cold and afraid without knowing why. He shrugged his shoulders and tried to dismiss the feeling telling himself that he was just tired and disappointed at the way things were going. The feeling and the look stayed with him for a few days and then settled into his subconciousness to perhaps surface at a latter date.

During the second lunchtime at school the following day there was great excitement at Spring Gardens High School. Mr. Sanders, the Mathematics teacher, had decided to go to a close neighbouring school, Chantille Hill, to do some school business and get back in time for his after lunch class. He normally parked his car in the shade of the pink poui, away from the main car park, to avoid the congestion and bother of getting out when he wanted to. As he approached, he noticed that the car seemed a bit low. He thought this strange and hastened towards it. On the playfield a little distance away, some students doing Physical Education were playing football. He paid them no attention. When he got to the car, his heart did a somer-sault. The four tyres were flat and the front wind shield had a crack which had widened like a peacock's plume or a semi-circular fan. For a while he stood transfixed with shock. He could not even utter a word. A teacher passed by and saw him standing and called to him. He did not respond in any way. The teacher thought it strange, certain that he had heard him and went up to him. He too stood rooted when he saw the destruction.

"What on earth is this?" he gasped. "Were you in an accident this morning?"

Mr. Sanders managed to mumble, "No." His eyes were still fixed on the car.

The teacher ran to the staff room and told everyone and then ran back to where Mr. Sanders was standing. Soon a crowd had gathered and everyone was talking excitedly.

Mr. Sanders did not join in, he had been rendered dumb. He moved towards the car when he saw a piece of paper imprisoned in one of the windshield wipers. He pulled it out. On it there was an exquisite drawing of a bird. It was coloured yellow and black. It was so life-like, it seemed as if it was about to fly off the paper. Mr. Sanders drew back; it was as if he could hear the wings pounding the air on its way to its mountain home. He examined it closely and made out some words which very cleverly formed a part of the drawing. It read 'Gold Eagle Power.'

Later on during the investigation, done by the Dean of Discipline, he tried to unearth the identity of the 'Gold Eagle Power.' No one had ever heard of such a person or gang before. It was the talk of the day. Even BJ and Brandon discussed the incident.

"My God BJ, what a cold yute! A wonder how him get to do that to Sir car without anybody seeing him! Him should call himself 'Mystic Operator' instead!" His voice was filled with awe and respect for the mysterious slick operator.

"Isn't he just powerful and cool, pulling off something like that right under everybody's nose?" BJ questioned quietly.

"You bet he is? Gosh he really is cold. I would not like to tangle with such a yute or gang," he said in awe.

"Well the best thing to do is not get yourself on anybody's wrong side. Some yute just hate when anybody at all, man, woman, child or beast mess with them. They make them pay," BJ answered with a distant look in his eyes.

When Juline heard about the incident she mused, "You see BJ was right. He must be very mean to the students why they would do that to him. It is not a nice thing but look at how he criticized BJ and me. He will not be so bright again. Serve him right."

CHAPTER 8

BJ'S STRANGE ILLNESS

Juline paced the floor uncomfortably. It was after eleven, and she still had not received the call to collect BJ from the party as yet. Since he had moved into grade nine he had received a number of invitations to parties. Bernard and herself had only allowed him to attend the ones from the upper classes, big names involved in large business ventures or who had financial clout. On this particular night, BJ was attending the birthday party of one of the boys in grade ten at his school. His father often did business with Bernard and had insisted that BJ celebrated his fifteenth birthday with him. The arrangement was that the parents would call the Hemmings when it was time for him to be picked up.

Bernard was fast asleep in his black massage chair. He did not see any reason why he should waste his time sitting up and worrying when he could claim some valuable sleep. Juline's feet carved a path in the carpet as she walked too and fro. When the clock said eleven thirty, Juline jerked him awake anxiously and persuaded him to start the journey to the Spartons. She could not wait any longer; BJ should have been home long ago in his bed.

When they arrived at the Spartons, they noticed that the activities were still in full swing; some young people were dancing to the loud pounding rhythmic reggae, some were playing pool and some eating and drinking. There were also couples wrapped up in themselves in secluded areas. They did not see BJ anywhere around. The dogs could be heard growling in the background. They searched for the Spartons in the crowd and finally found them on the back porch simply sitting around, leaving the fast pace to the young people.

When the Hemmings enquired for BJ, Mr. Sparton was surprised and told them that he had told BJ to use the telephone in the den to call them from quarter to eleven. He thought they had been busy and had only just got the time to get him.

They started walking around asking everyone if they had seen BJ. Everyone said he had been there up to an hour before then he had disappeared. They thought he had gone home. The Hemmings and the Spartons became very concerned. Juline was almost beside herself with fear. She somehow had a peculiar feeling that something was wrong. A nervous ache formed at the bottom of her abdomen and as it grew, worked its way into her limbs, and lodged itself into her head. It was a cool night and the community of Delmeade was generally thought of as being salubrious, but Juline was sweating copiously.

Bernard decided to search the house and the extensive grounds of the Sparton's house. The dogs who had been locked in their kennels before the party started, barked furiously at the strangers. Outside the trees seemed tall, dark and menacing. The wind rattled through them, causing them to quiver and dip like Juline's feeling. There were some large clumps of plants and they examined each hollering out BJ's name. The search of the grounds yielded nothing and then someone suggested the swimming pool. Some of the boys who could swim, undressed to their underwear and jumped into the pool, as soon as the light which covered the whole pool area was turned on. It was while they were searching that a shout was heard from an area behind the kennel. Everyone had kept away from the kennel area because of the aggressive, threatening barks of the dogs.

It was Shomare, the Sparton's son, whose party was being held, who had made the shout. He had noticed that the dogs had seemed extremely restive during the latter part of the night. Crowds and parties were no strange things to them, and he had never heard them behave in such an agitated manner before, so he had gone to investigate, certain that something was wrong. He was not expecting to stumble over a form lying behind the kennel.

He gave a loud shout, "Over here! Over here! I think I have found him." His voice held excitement and disbelief.

Juline felt something wet coursing down her legs but she paid no attention to it. She was one of the first persons to reach the area behind the kennel. "BJ! BJ! My baby!" she bawled out in a frightening manner. "BJ, BJ, what game are you playing. Wake up!" she bent over him and took his head in her hands.

"BJ, are you okay?" This came from Bernard, who was by now kneeling beside him.

BJ laid still, his handsome face looked pallid and drained of blood. There was a swelling at the left side of his neck just below his ear. When his father felt the area, blood covered his hand. He felt for his pulse and found that he was still breathing.

"Someone call the ambulance and the police," he gasped frantically.

Juline got up, and then she knelt beside him and bawled holding her belly. "Jesus Christ, somebody kill mi son. Jesus Christ him dead! Dead! Dead! Bernard, them kill you one boy! Jesus Christ, come down! BJ, wake up and talk to me! Wake up and tell me that you not dead!" She laid prostrate on him and had to be pulled off.

"Juline he's not dead, but you will kill him if you continue to lie on him," Bernard said, trying hard not to break down; his wife was already on the edge of collapsing and it would not do to have both of them in the same condition.

They tried to move BJ, but stopped after they had moved him only a few inches when somebody told them to leave him alone until the ambulance came. After they had rested him again on the ground somebody said, "Look he must have hit his head on this stone when he fell!" everyone gathered around to look.

"But what was he doing around here by himself?" somebody asked. Everybody listened, hoping that some-one would supply an answer to that mystery.

"You were all here at the party," Juline said, close to hysterics, "so how come nobody don't know what happen to him and why he was here by himself? Somebody must do something to him and him run come down here so," she added emphatically, certain that she was right.

"Juline, we don't know that yet. It looks strange, but we don't know, so we can't start making allegations," Bernard's prudent voice cautioned. "Let us wait and see, the doctors and the police will decide that."

Meanwhile, Mr. Sparton was trying to revive BJ with smelling salts, but he laid comatose. Juline walked away from the crowd, heedless of the dogs ceaseless barking. She held on to a tree and vomited until she thought her entrails would come through her mouth. She groaned over and over unable to cry, her salivary gland must have dried up, she thought. Her head felt like a big round ball of nothing, when she touched it, it didn't even seem to be there. Some-body came over to her and helped her back to the scene of her agony.

Soon the ambulance and the police came. They lifted BJ's motionless body and placed him in the ambulance. His parents went with him. Juline sat with him, while Bernard sat at the front.

Juline was not someone who did much praying. She believed that there was a God, as her God fearing parents had instilled in her, but she had neglected Him or used Him only when there was a need. She felt that there was a need at that moment and started to pray aloud, "Dear God, I know I don't always pray but that does not mean that I don't believe in you. Right now Jesus, I need your help. Please let BJ live, Lord. Don't let him die because you know how much I love him. If he dies, I know I am going to die too. Lord, I don't want any of us to die. I promise that I will send him to church if he lives. Jesus Christ, please help me. And, Lord, help me find the one who hurt him."

Sitting at the front, Bernard could not hear every word Juline was saying, but he knew she was praying. "Was she trying to bribe God?" he criticized to himself. BJ was his only son, but he could not do what Juline was doing. From his knowledge of God, he knew he was not someone to play with; so he wouldn't try to play with Him. He would just have to trust that He would see it fit to save his one boy. It was at that moment that he realized, that Jared and other family members were not aware of what was happening, so one by one starting with Jared he called them. He told Jared not to come to the hospital but to stay at home until he was contacted.

At the hospital, BJ was rushed into Emergency. His parents waited outside, hopeful and anxious. Juline almost pushed Bernard into the realm of craziness with her constant pacing, muttering and crying. Her tear ducts had been replenished, and she was raining tears. He tried to hug her to keep her calm but she pushed him away and continued her routine.

"Juline for heaven's sake sit down for a while. If you collapse there's no way I am going to be able to take care of two people. Sit down for heaven's sake!" he ordered, trying to calm her. "You are stressing me out and have been doing so for some time now."

"This is a good time for you to curse me off. A very good time. Hit me when I am low!" she cried, hurt to the heart about what she considered Bernard's unfair comments. She had noticed for months now that he seemed distracted when he was with her. He was not as jovial as usual and sometimes he came in later than usual. He was also doing more travelling abroad, giving the excuse of increased business. He also seemed to be against BJ, he rarely took his part in any of the little scrapes he got into.

She used the opportunity to hit out against him. "I am stressed by you too. You don't seem to be interested in BJ anymore. Every little thing is a problem to you. You always give him wrong and give everybody else right. You don't try to understand him at all. You always want to punish him. You even treat Jared better than him sometimes. As for me, you get tired a me now! Home late, gone abroad every minute, ignore me!" she stopped as she was out of breath. She was breathing hard and Bernard felt sorry for her. He tried to hug her again but she pushed him away again.

"When all this is over I will deal with all your comments. You have said a lot and I have a lot to say too. But let it wait. Let it wait."

As he sat down, a doctor appeared. He jumped up expectant, "How is he Doc? Is he going to be okay?" he asked anxiously, looking into the doctor's eyes.

"Well, Mr. Hemmings, is it?" he started then went on without confirmation of the name, "his breathing has stabilized now but he still seems to be in a coma. We are running some tests to try and determine exactly what is happening. The results will not be ready until tomorrow evening so I suggest that you go home and get some sleep." The doctor having said his piece turned to go.

"But, Doctor, what about the cut in his head back, how did he get that?" Juline asked not satisfied with the scanty information.

"He seems to have fallen and hit his head, but as I said tomorrow we will have more definite answers." With that he left, leaving the Hemmings to discuss what they had heard.

"Well let us go home, Juline. There is nothing more we can do here. We have to leave the doctors and nurses to do their job," Bernard said, rising to go.

Juline sat down on a nearby chair. With fire blazing in her eyes she accused, "You see how quickly you want to abandon our son? You see how quickly you want to leave him alone? I am staying right here! You can go if you want to. If he wakes up in the night and needs me I will be right here for him," she said stubbornly, not budging.

"Well, Juline," Bernard said, getting out his phone and calling a taxicab, "I am tired and my head is near to exploding. If I don't get a little rest, I am going to end up here too. I can feel my blood pressure rising and I don't want it to get worse. Come home ,you need to rest too," he pleaded, hoping that she would give in.

Juline was adamant, "If you want to leave go. I was the one who bear the pain and bring him here and if he is going out I will go with him," she pouted and sat where she was.

Without saying anything else, Bernard left. Juline could hardly believe her eyes. He had left her alone just like that as if BJ did not matter. "When did the novelty of having an only son wear off?" she wondered. Was it because the boy acted like a healthy fourteen year old and not like a retired maiden? "Well I will stay here, she decreed to herself. I will do anything for my son."

At about two o'clock, the nurse on duty went into the waiting area and saw Juline hunched over a chair. She wondered who she was and why she was still there but decided against waking her for the information.

Before dawn when the hospital was very still, Juline woke up wondering why she wasn't stretched out beside Bernard in their king-sized bed. As the past night's events revisited her memory, she gave a yelp like a wounded dog and then covered her mouth. She tiptoed towards the direction which they had taken BJ and started looking in every room.

She soon found the room and hastily tiptoed towards the bed. Once there, she touched his hand and his face, but apart from the heaving of the chest there was no sign of life. He looked pathetic lying there with all sorts of tubes attached to his hands and other parts of his body. She was afraid of touching him too hard lest any of the tubes were shifted. She stood there for a long time, just watching him and remembering his vibrancy, exuberance and mood swings. It was only when she heard approaching feet that she dodged out of the room and tiptoed back to the waiting area. She cried herself to sleep and woke up only when Bernard, Jared, her parents and one of Bernard's aunt and brother came in and woke her up.

Despite the manner in which they had parted, she was glad to see everyone. It was a sombre gathering, and no one was in the mood for much talking. Bernard asked permission from one of the nurses to allow Juline to bathe and change. She looked really dishevelled, and after all that vomiting and urine she really welcomed the opportunity.

They all stayed until the doctor had seen all the patients on the ward, but he had no additional information to give them, as the tests results would not be in until late afternoon. The family sat around not speaking much. Juline called her work place to explain her absence, and Jared knew there would be no school for him that day.

In the late afternoon, the doctor who had been on call the night before called the Hemmings into his office and told them to sit down. Juline, expecting the worse, started sobbing. Bernard reached over and held her hand, and this time she did not push him away. Whatever it was, she needed strength and support.

The doctor looked keenly at both parents. He noted their expensive dress and sophisticated air and immediately labelled them as thriving middle class. More and more of this class seemed to be having problems with their children in one way or the other. He quickly summed up the situation, over-indulgent parents, spoilt child not receiving enough firmness and attention, maybe allowed to run wild.

"Where did you say your son was before you brought him in?" the doctor questioned.

"He was at a birthday party for one of my friend's son," Bernard volunteered, wondering what the question had to do with his son's illness.

"Does he always go to parties?" the doctor continued his questioning, leaning towards the couple with interest.

This time Juline answered. "We normally select the ones that he goes to. We always meet the family beforehand."

The doctor continued his probing, "And which school does he attend? Does he have many friends there?" He leaned even closer to them.

"Well," Bernard took back the baton. "He attends Spring Gardens High and he has quite a few friends." He was tired of the questions and wanted to hear the news which he was certain was bad.

"Well Sir, your son seemed to have fallen in with a bad lot or a bad lot has fallen in with him," he announced solemnly.

Before Bernard who was leaning closer to him could ask him anything else, he delivered the news. "Your son is suffering from an overdose of drugs," he reported calmly, as if he were telling the time.

"What?" Bernard jumped up knocking over his chair. "You mean that the boy is on drugs. Dear Jesus, drugs! Drugs! How did this happen? Hell, how do I tell anyone this? Jesus…" he stopped talking as he heard a thud behind him. Juline had slumped to the floor; she had fainted.

The doctor rushed outside and called a nurse, while Bernard shouted her name. "Juline, Jule wake up! Juline, Jule!" his efforts were wasted.

The doctor and the nurse rushed back in followed by an orderly with a stretcher. Bernard and the orderly placed her on the stretcher and the orderly wheeled her away, followed by the doctor and the nurse.

Bernard was left standing alone on the corridor. Before he could decide what to do all those who were there to visit BJ rushed towards him. They had heard the commotion and had seen Juline passing on the stretcher. Her mother was in tears and demanded to know what had happened to her daughter.

"What is wrong with Juline? Dear God, first BJ and now my child? What is happening to this family?" she cried, wringing her hands and flinging them up into the air, petitioning God to give her the answer.

"Juline will be fine mother," Bernard responded. "She only faint, she will soon come around."

"But what cause her to faint like that?" Jared questioned perplexed. "First BJ, now Mummy… this is too much!" He put his hands on his head and looked up to heaven.

"What wrong wid BJ, Bernard, cause that must be why she faint?" asked Juline's father, Frank Bond.

Bernard did not answer right away. How could he face this disgrace after he had boasted so much about his son to everyone? He had made certain that he kept BJ's misdeeds at home. No one knew of the little problems at home and school.

"Bernard, you have to tell us," said his brother. "We are all family and sooner or later we have to hear so you might as well tell us now," he repeated looking hard at Bernard.

When Bernard broke the news, everyone stood without saying a word. The whole thing was inconceivable, Bernard's son taking drugs. It sounded shocking and sad. No one knew what to say or how they would tell anyone about this. Jared thought that if BJ died it would be easier for them because then they could hide the truth. But BJ did not die.

CHAPTER 9

❧❀❧❀❀❧❧❀❀❧❧❀❀❧❀

MR. HEMMINGS' ACCIDENT

It was three months after that fateful night when BJ had overdosed. He had been placed in a detoxification programme and was ready to go back home and start attending school. He had been grilled for hours by the police who wanted to find out where he had obtained the drugs, who else was involved in the habit and where and when he took the drugs. He refused to answer any of the questions, claiming that somebody at the party had placed the drugs in his food and he didn't know who it was. The police had a meeting with all the parents whose children had attended the party and encouraged them to have their children tested. This did not go down well with some of the parents, but at the police's insistence most of them complied. The results were shocking as eight out of the thirty boys were found to be drug abusers. Their parents' trust and complacency were flattened. Not one of them had placed any special significance on the symptoms of withdrawal, vacant looks, mood swings and loss of interest in some activities.

Juline claimed that BJ had always been that way. She infuriated Bernard by believing BJ's every word especially about the drugs being placed in his food. As Mr. Sparton's son had also been discovered to be a drug abuser, she blamed him for doping BJ and kept her distance from the Spartons. Bernard upbraided her for this and asked her if it was the Sparton boy who had smuggled the small amount of drugs he had found in BJ's room, when he had searched it the day after the doctor's news. She was at a loss and commanded him not to tell anyone. Bernard pointed out to her, that whereas he was going to support every effort to get BJ back to normal, he was not going to support any form of illegal activity in his house. He threatened to turn him over to the law if he did not behave himself.

"What, you would turn over your own son to the police?" Juline questioned, glaring at him.

"Try me and see. While I blame myself for some of what has happened, I am not going to support him in wrong doing. From now on things around here are going to change. For one, I will only give him enough money for lunch and a snack. Two, he will not attend any more parties. Three, I am going to sell the horse and fourthly, he will get himself involved in extra-curricular activities after school instead of hanging around with rotten eggs like himself."

"Why don't you just kill him instead?" Juline asked, fixing Bernard with a withering look. "The only things I agree with you about are the parties and getting involved in sports. But why take away the horse he loves so much and lessen his allowance?" she questioned, trying to wilt him.

She failed and his next statement showed it, "When a child has too much money to spend, he uses it to do foolishness. He used his money to buy drugs, excess money he got from you, me and other family members. Money that should have been put in the bank was given to this boy to do foolishness. I will try to curb this." Bernard spoke as one who had made up his mind.

"How do you know he bought any drugs? Didn't you hear the boy say he didn't buy any drugs?" she put in lamely.

"I agree with you," said Bernard. "They love him so much that they use their money to buy drugs and then just give him like that." He was being sarcastic and she knew it. "Another thing is that we have pampered the boy too much, buying him everything he asks for. No wonder the boy who has such a good brain think that him mustn't do much at school. Why should he work when he can get every wretched thing him want? You know how hard me had to work through school, through university so I could get into business and make a life for myself?" He looked harshly at Juline to underscore his words.

"Yes, but when parents work hard it is normally for their children so that their lives can be better than theirs," she countered triumphantly.

"I agree, but remember, mother have, father have, blessed is the child that have for himself. Whether is so or not that is how it will be." His tone showed his determination and showed that he would brook no opposition.

BJ did not attend school for a whole term and before he went back his father placed the new laws before him. He did not respond in any way, instead he fixed him with another of those chilling looks, which made Bernard uncomfortable.

BJ went back to school after his father had persuaded the principal to accept him back. They both had to sign a long sheet of regulations. In addition to this, the principal made it clear that if he did anything serious, he would be expelled. Bernard had to sign to this as well.

It was strange, but BJ now enjoyed more popularity than he did before. Heroism had been thrust upon him while he was lying in the hospital. He was especially admired for not divulging his drug sources to the police or his parents. He was sought after by both sexes, but he wisely kept aloof while he basked in the popularity. Brandon remained his friend. He admired BJ, but somewhere inside him, there was fear of him. Sometimes the look in BJ's eyes caused him to ruminate about some of the things he said and did. Brandon thought it was best to be BJ's friend instead of his enemy, but despite that decision, he kept an inward wary eye on BJ.

BJ settled into school and tried to keep his mind on his lessons, but it was a difficult undertaking. His spending power was curtailed, and his fun was severely hampered by his father's restrictions and this displeased him. All the parties were passing him by; he had to depend on vicarious information and pictures that were passed around in his circle. His precious horse, Black Eagle, had been sold and so was his equestrian dreams. His father had become a police officer and a preacher; all he did was watch and counsel, peep and admonish. BJ felt like a detainee at home. Life had become dull and not worthwhile.

One morning during the last term in grade ten, just as he settled in for his first class for the day, there was an announcement on the school's intercom immediately summoning him to the principal's office. When he got there; his uncle who operated the motor vehicle business with his father and one of his father's sister that he barely knew were waiting there. Their faces were glum and tense. It was obvious that they had been crying. They told BJ to sit and enquired after his health and schooling.

His uncle then cleared his throat and without looking at BJ he began, "I'm afraid I have bad news for you. This morning after you left for school, your father was driving to work when his SUV crashed. It went right over into the gully down the road from his home. He is badly injured and the vehicle is written off." He stopped speaking and then searched BJ's face for a reaction.

BJ received his uncle's news with silence. His expression remained unchanged and indefinable. It could have been that the words had not reached him or that he did not fully understand the information. He seemed to be in another world.

After a long silence he asked, "Where is he now?"

"He is in the St. Mark Hospital," his aunt answered, wondering at the boy's capacity to remain serene in the face of bad news.

"And where is my mother?" was BJ's next question.

"She and Jared and other family members are with him at the hospital," she answered, then added, "We have come for you, the principal has given us permission for you to leave with us."

The principal gave BJ a note to take to his teacher, and he left for the classroom. He did not walk very fast, but sauntered to the bathroom first, then stood at the water cooler in a very pensive manner. Finally, he made his way to the classroom and then gave the teacher the note.

She read it and exclaimed, "Good God," and then enquired sympathetically, "Are you alright?"

"Yes, Miss. I'm fine," BJ answered in a polite and charming voice. "I'm leaving now, Miss." He picked up his bag and left the classroom, his teacher's sympathetic eyes following him.

When BJ arrived at the hospital, his mother hugged him, "Thank God you are okay," she purred giving the impression that he too had been hurt. Her eyes were swollen with crying, her hair was in disarray, and her cream and plum linen suit was soiled. To her it was déjà vu. Juline felt that her world was no longer secure, first BJ's unfortunate episode and now Bernard. He had sustained so many injuries that they were not certain whether he would live. She had never conceived this ever happening to her husband. This was certainly not the life she had planned. Everything seemed to have become unglued and was falling apart around her. She had not kept her bargain with God when BJ had survived his illness so she was afraid to approach Him. Moreover, this seemed to be His way of getting back at her. But despite her reasoning, she cried out, "Lord, duh don't let him die! Duh, Lord, duh!"

"God will help him," said his father. "God will help him." He looked old and tired as if he too were ready to fall apart like his son's life.

Jared kept quiet and tried to keep close to his mother most of the time. He was afraid that she was going to collapse. She looked just as sick as she had when she came out of the hospital after BJ's episode. Mentally, he had not yet got over the pain and embarrassment that BJ had caused the family. He had been especially sorry for his stepfather because he had tried a little to check BJ's behaviour. Even though he loved his mother, he had serious objections about the way she over-indulged BJ and the manner in which she always wanted to blame him for his misdeeds. He knew that he was a distant second in her affections, even though he did not give her half as many problems as BJ did. He believed it had something to do with his father or some other thing from his past that he was oblivious of. He also had his suspicions about some things which had happened in the house, but with the wisdom of Solomon, he kept his eyes cleverly averted and his mouth glued shut.

While everyone waited in anguish outside, Bernard laid in the emergency room, swathed in bandages like an exaggerated cartoon figure. There were gashes and open cuts everywhere. He had suffered head injuries and his face was like a stripped ripe cherry. He had broken his left arm, a number of ribs and his right leg. If he ever survived he would certainly not be the striking husband Juline had adored. At the moment she really was only wishing for his survival. Even more than BJ, he had tubes attached to his body. He looked like a mannequin (which had lost its glory) stiff, supine and silent. He would be the only one able to tell his story if he lived. No other vehicle was involved in the accident; no one knew what had really happened.

Bernard was hospitalized for two whole months. He underwent a number of operations, with each one bringing him closer and closer to life. For a little more than a month he was unable to speak or move. Then gradually a few indistinct words came along with life feebly coursing back into his body. The doctor explained to his family that he would never be able to speak and walk as he did before the accident. Juline was elated that Bernard was going to survive the accident; but the doctor's words painted a picture of a handicapped man, who would not be able to get around much and would virtually be a baby again.

Juline discussed her predicament with one of her friends at work. "But Marcy, how am I going to manage in a situation like that?" she blurted out.

"It going to be difficult, but when he is released you just have to stay home for a while and take care of him."

"I know that, but how am I still going to manage! He is such a big man and moving him is going to break my back."

"But Juline, don't you have two big boys in the house and other family members?" Marcy asked, trying to make sense of Juline's concern.

"Yes, but they will be at school most of the day," she answered.

"What about the helper? Couldn't you pay her extra and get her to live in until the crisis is over? Surely you mus' can work out something," Marcy thought that Juline, who was always boasting about her husband and their child, was really not a strong person in times of trouble. It was like she wanted to run away from the responsibility of nursing her husband.

"Well, I suppose I have to manage and still find time for the rest of my family, especially the last boy. I need to spend time with him," she said.

"I thought you said that the strange sickness that the boy had clear up now. By the way, the doctors did really find out what wrong with him? Is it something that is going to keep coming back?" Marcy enquired, concerned that two sick persons would indeed be too much for Juline.

"BJ is okay now," Juline answered quickly, not wanting to discuss BJ's strange illness with anyone, especially somebody who was not a member of the family. She had told everyone at work that BJ had a strange illness. She did not go into any details, and people had formed their own opinion about the nature of the illness; their diagnosis ranged from different forms of cancer, to mild forms of mental illnesses. Many of them understood Juline not wanting to discuss any illness of this magnitude, but a few thought she was stupid since anybody could have any kind of illness, and since illnesses were not selected and purchased at the market.

"Well, since he is okay I don't see the big problem; everybody should pitch in and help."

Juline did not tell anyone how afraid she was to be alone with Bernard. He would never be the same again. The physical change was evident to everyone, and it was quite understandable that there would be some amount of emotional change, but Juline had sensed something else. The relationship had started to become a little strange and strained especially after BJ's overdose. She felt that somehow Bernard blamed her for what had happened and that he did not love BJ, their own child, her son, anymore. The last argument they had before his accident rushed back to her. He had come in about twelve o'clock that night from work. She had gone downstairs when she heard his SUV drive in and sat waiting for him in the living room. She sharpened her claws and pounced on him as soon as he opened the door. "Do you know what time it is?" she questioned, as if speaking to one of her boys.

"Good night to you too," said Bernard, spinning around to meet the caustic voice.

"Good night, good night, it is not night anymore. Didn't they tell you at school what twelve at this time means?" she fired back, looking at him steadily, hoping to see some form of remorse in his eyes. But his look was unwavering as he matched her gaze.

"I really do not have the time for the argument now. I am tired and would love to get some sleep," he replied, moving past her and going up the stairs.

"Tired! Tired of doing what? Drinking, going out with another woman, hiding away from home and your responsibility?" She rose from her seat and edged closer to him, waiting for him to answer.

"I see you have left out taking drugs," he said quietly. "Do you want to know which of them I am taking?" His voice had a deadly, steely quality to it, as he came back down the stairs and faced her.

Juline knew that the drug reference was an indirect slap referring to BJ's problem. Bernard was still angry at the deep humiliation the boy had caused him and used either silence or indirect references to remind her about it. And to think, thought Juline, the boy was set up! Given drugs by somebody else and his father instead of supporting him was against both herself and the boy. "If he did anything wrong you are to be blamed just like me!" she retorted.

"Well, even so, you support him in every wrong. When I try to discipline him you don't like it or you go behind my back and pamper him. One ah dis fine day him going to nyam off you ears dem or put you in prison!" he shouted, reverting to the emphatic Creole to cement his point.

"Well, ah mi bring him come here an' I will go out wid him!" Juline shouted back, also using the vernacular to match his passion. "An' you keep coming in here late cause you find more fun out a road!" she added. "One of these nights, I am going to lock this door from the inside and you can go back where you coming from!"

When Bernard dropped his case, grabbed Juline and raised his hand to hit her, she realized that she had gone too far. In all their fifteen years together, he had never raised his hand at her, much more to hit her. She was too shocked to react and could only stare at him. Sanity shot back into Bernard's head and jerked him back to reality. Suddenly, he released Juline and stepped away from her, as if she were the attacker and he the attacked. When he had retreated far enough, he pointed his finger straight at her. "If you ever try to keep me out of my house, that my life blood, toil and tears buy and pay for, you are the one who will find yourself outside. This is my castle and I reign in here not you!"

By this time he was shouting loudly and was shaking all over as if he had been suddenly struck with Alzheimer's disease. He took up his attaché and tramped upstairs passing BJ and Jared on the landing without even acknowledging them. He did not even respond to Jared's, "Good night Dad."

Since then, Iceland came to reside in the Hemmings' household. There were no more arguments, only polite, necessary conversations in front of the children and visitors.

When they were not around, the ice settled and hardened again.

Two weeks after, Bernard had the accident. When he came out of the coma he could not remember anyone, or anything. The faces simply came and went and when the police tried to question him, he stared at them vacantly. The doctor announced that he had been hit with amnesia. When his mother repeated her name and his name, he only looked at her blankly, as if from far away. One day at the hospital, when BJ thought that no one was seeing him; he went and stood over his father's silent form and made a funny face and stuck out his tongue. The observer thought of calling him and rebuking him but thought better of it. Rather, the person stored the inexplicable behaviour for future thought and reference.

Bernard's amnesia lasted for five weeks. One day, the nurse on duty heard a thud inside his room and rushed inside. Bernard was lying on the ground calling for help. None of his family was around, so the nurse rushed outside again calling for help.

After he had been placed on the bed, he asked the nurse, "Where am I? Who brought me here?" His speech was laboured and low.

The nurse sensing that something had changed asked him, "What is your name?"

"Bernard, Bernard Hemmings," he replied with much effort, breathing heavily as if he had just completed an arduous race.

The nurse rushed out and called the doctor who dashed in quickly and questioned him, "What is your name? Do you have any children? What are their names? What is your occupation?" Bernard answered all the questions correctly according to the doctor's knowledge, and he knew the patient had fought his way out of the forest and was now in the clearing.

Bernard's family was elated when later that evening they found out for themselves. His father and his mother started a conversation about a friend they had to visit in another hospital when Bernard asked, "Whas wrong with Misser Lynsh mother?"

At first they just stood staring with disbelief, then his father asked, "Son, what is your name?"

"Berrnarrrd Hemmings," he replied.

His mother clapped her hand and hugged her husband. "Thank God! Thank God, he is remembering, he is remembering!" She rushed to tell the nurse, who simply smiled and told her that they knew, but wanted them to find out for themselves.

When Juline and the boys arrived at the hospital the same trick was done to them. Juline and Jared were euphoric, but BJ only gave a small smile which did not reach his eyes or spread across his whole face, it stopped at the corner of his mouth.

Two days after the police came to question him about the accident. "Mr. Hemmings, are you certain that you can remember the details of what happened?" the more senior of the two officer asked as if he were asking a lost child for particulars.

"Yes, I can," Bernard answered. He most certainly could; because as soon as his memory had returned fully, the horror of that fateful morning plagued his mind, even when he was sleeping. His days and nights were one continuous nightmare, a CD placed on repeat that went over and over in his mind.

"Can you tell us what happened?" the junior officer interrupted his thoughts, bringing him back to the present.

"Not much to tell," Bernard stated. "I got in the carrr and when I starrrted it and plashed my feet on the brakesh I knew shomthing was wrong." He paused as if he were tired and the senior officer prompted, "What do you mean when you said something was wrong?" he questioned, leaning forward.

"The brakesh just did not feel right. It felt slack and uncomfortable," he recounted, with a distant look in his eyes.

"Why didn't you come out and check it?" the junior officer wanted to find out.

"I wash already laash for work and I didn't thinksh mush of it," he paused again and a look appeared on his patchwork face which said if only I had. "Ash soon ash I gosh throughsh my gate, my SUV gosh out of control." He paused again, reliving the accident in his mind.

The officers waited a while before prompting him again. The nurse on duty had warned them that his speech would be laborious and unclear at times and they should be patient. They were advised that if they tried to harass him in any way they would be asked to leave.

"Do you remember what happened afterwards?" the senior officer asked kindly, almost enunciating as if Mr. Hemmings did not quite understand English. He leaned forward again waiting on him to restart.

"Do I remember, you meansh can Ish ever forgetsh. The SUV jush sped along narrowly misshing other vehicles and then it rusht through the stoplight and dived into the gully. Then everythinsh went black and blanksh," he finished, exhausted and closed his eyes as if the accident had happened again, and he was lying unconsciously in the gully.

Before responding, the senior officer glanced at the report again, checking for some form of corroboration from it. "Mr. Hemmings," he addressed Bernard, closing the report, "your family asked the mechanic to check your car after the accident and they found that the brakes had been meddled with." He stopped and allowed the information to sink in, watching the eyes in the patchwork widen and then return to normal. "Were you having any problems on your way home the night before the accident?" he queried.

"Nosh, everything wash okay," Bernard replied.

"Did anybody at home use the vehicle after you parked it?" the junior officer asked.

"Nosh, everybody at home drivesh their own vehicle. Nobodysh drivesh my SUV," he replied, a look of consternation appearing on his face. His brain was still sharp and he could follow the line of questioning. He knew exactly what the officer was getting at.

"We would like to question the members of your immediate family," the officer revealed. "When will that be possible?"

"They comesh here almost every day, so you cansh come back after five," he said.

"One last thing," the senior officer added, "who goes by the name 'Gold Eagle Power'?"

"I have never hearst of sush a person. Why do you askst?"

"Someone found an exquisite drawing of an eagle and the name 'Gold Eagle Power,' which was part of the drawing in your SUV."

"Never heardst of sush a thing," Mr. Hemmings replied.

After the police had questioned Juline and the children, she was bursting with anger. She remarked to her parents later, "They were literally saying that one of the three of us had tampered with the SUV! What a piece of effrontery! Why would anybody want to hurt Bernard? Poor BJ, he was so outraged to be questioned like a criminal. A wonder if they think my little boy know anything bout car to do something like that? Somebody mus' break in the garage or something but not us, especially BJ who love him father so much!"

CHAPTER 10

JARED LEAVES HOME

When Tara-Ann heard of her father's accident she was very depressed. Despite what had happened on her last visit, she still loved her father. Unknown to anyone else she had gone to her father's business place and had tried to convince him of her innocence. Mr. Hemmings had been confused because he had found the money in her suitcase himself. He believed in her and could not fathom why she would want to steal when he provided very well for her and his other children. He had a special position in his heart for her and wished he could erase the disconsolate look she was wearing in her eyes. It was not a good thing for someone so young to be beset with such a burden. He had told her to forget it and he would too, but she told him that one day he would find out the truth and that would remove all remnants of suspicion from his mind.

She had gone to the hospital to visit him on more than one occasions, taking care that she did not meet BJ and her stepmother. When she learnt that her father had left the hospital, she was at a loss as to how her visits could be continued. She did not want any confrontation, but she wanted to spend some time with her father. She wanted to help dispel the loneliness and despair she had sensed were stealing over him. After all, it was a daughter's duty to care for her father, especially one who was not living with her but had shown so much interest and had been so kind. Without his wife's knowledge, Mr. Hemmings had shown up on a number of occasions at his three daughters' consultation days at school, had visited or called on their birthdays and sometimes on special holidays or events. He also made it a habit to call them at different times to speak to them. They all knew that this was not enough, but it was better than maintenance money without a father.

Tara-Ann decided that whatever the outcome, she was going to visit her father. It was her sincere prayer that Betty would be the only one present when she got there but this was not to be. She was sweating with fear by the time the taxi stopped at the front gate. She knew she could not just walk through the gates because it was automatically operated, and then there was the matter of the dogs, so she called her father's cellular phone. "Hello, Daddy it's me, Tara-Ann, and I am standing outside the gate," she announced.

"Betty will come and opensh it for you," he said.

Although his wife was sitting in the living room reading a magazine, he did not tell her that Tara-Ann was outside, but rang the bell for Betty.

"What do you want, Bernard?" she asked, surprised that she was sitting right there and he had rung for Betty.

"Itsh all right," he muttered, not looking at her. When Betty arrived he told her, "Let in the pershon at the gate quickly."

"Yes, Sir," replied Betty, moving away immediately.

Juline followed her to the door to see who it was. Bernard noticed her action and called to her, "Dontsh you say onesh word to her, not even onesh!" The harsh look he gave her underlined his order. Partially disabled or not, he was still in charge in his house.

To say that Juline was shocked when she saw Tara-Ann following Betty up the walkway was putting it moderately! She had hoped that none of Bernard's girls would ever set foot through her gate again. Didn't the girl have any shame or what? Why should she return to the scene of her crime, the thieving opportunist? Whom did she wish to impress with her false show of filial duty? It had been about four years now since the revealing incident and since she had last seen the girl, and Juline could not help but notice how much more beautiful the girl had become. Her dark skin shone with health and she moved with the grace of a cultured young lady. Juline imagined that members of the opposite sex would turn to stare whenever she honoured them with her presence. She felt a spasm of jealousy, knowing that despite the unfortunate incident of four years before, this girl had unseated BJ in her father's affection. Juline hated her even more than before. In her absence the hatred was abstract; with her present it was a sharp reality. No usurper should have misplaced BJ in her husband's heart. Even if Bernard did not love her as before, his only son should always be number one, how dare this bastard wheedle her way in with her sophisticated speech and attitude? Well, good English and bearing or not, she was a thief and her boy was not! He was a decent, well-bred boy that some people chose to misunderstand, but she would stand by him, no matter what.

Tara-Ann saw her stepmother standing at the door and her heart dipped and lowered itself into her shoes. Maybe it would be better if she turned back, she argued to herself. It would not help to make a bad situation worse. Above all things, her father needed peace and comfort to help with the healing process, not more confusion and discomfort. She was making up her mind to turn around when a male voice called out, "Come inshide, Tara." Her father had hopped to the door on his crutches and was waiting there for her.

"Good morning, Daddy, Good morning, Mrs. Hemmings," a grateful Tara-Ann greeted both, glad for her father's presence at the door.

"Good morning, my daughter," said Mr. Hemmings, feeling so good for the first time that morning that his mended face broke out into a grin.

"Good morning, Tara-Ann," Juline answered grudgingly, not even bothering to look at her.

"Comest and sit wish me, Tara. Imst happy to see you." He hopped over to his recliner. She took his crutches from him and then assisted him onto the recliner. She then went and got a chair and sat close to him. She could feel her stepmother's eyes piercing into her like needles, but she averted her eyes and paid full attention to her father. Since he could not speak very clearly; he raised the topics for conversation and allowed her to do most of the discussion. His face was transformed from boredom to rapt interest, as he listened to Tara's discourse on different issues. She had now finished upper sixth form and was awaiting exam results for entry into university. She had opted to stay at home instead of going abroad to study, and her father was somehow glad about it. If she did not get the required grades she would do a first degree in Arts and then follow up with Law school. Listening to her, he had no doubt that she would qualify from her examinations; she was so incisive and her skills of analysis were remarkable.

Juline listened for a while. They did not include her in the conversation, and she did not seek entry into it. She thought the girl was showing off the little knowledge she had acquired, but deep down there was envious admiration for the way she spoke. If things were different around here that's how BJ would be speaking and reasoning and keeping company with his father. Instead of the schooled tolerance on his face when he spoke to BJ, there would be animated interest like what he now showed when talking to Tara. She stole away stealthily, almost scuttling up the stairs. Bernard pretended he did not see her. He was very amused by her actions. The temperature would certainly normalize with the absence of her cloudy presence and it would give them a chance to talk more freely.

It was Tara's plan to get away in the early afternoon before BJ came home. Jared was fine, but BJ could be so unpleasant at times. She hoped that the taxi she had called would come before they arrive. Her plan was thwarted by a thunderstorm, which came without much warning. At one moment, the sun was smiling pleasantly across the sky, and then unprovoked it broke out into a scowl, which got darker and blacker rapidly. It was soon accompanied by fierce, shouting thunder, which zipped and tore across the sky frenetically. The two induced the presence of the rain, which came out of hiding and gushed down in a purposeful manner, drenching everything in its fury. Tara-Ann watched the plants bowing and kneeling as they wept copiously. They tried to stand upright at times, but the rain swept them back on their knees to do penance.

When the violence of the rain had subsided, Tara-Ann stood by the window watching small streams of water strolling along happily, only to be later pulled into the greedy earth. She heard vehicles swishing and hitting the water on the road, and then one turned in at the gate. It did not come through the gate but stopped, and two boys emerged. Tara-Ann's heart started working overtime when she realized that it was BJ and Jared. As they walked up the driveway, she could not help noticing how well they had grown. BJ seemed to be competing with Jared in height. He was a tall and handsome boy with a very serious expression on his face. He had the bearing of an athlete, and Tara-Ann wondered if he was actively involved in sports. Jared, walking behind him, was no less handsome. He bore a sober serene and scholarly look, which was emphasized by the glasses he wore.

Tara-Ann stood where she was, not knowing where to move to. The rain had lulled her father to sleep, and she had no wish to wake him up to protect her from BJ's unfriendliness. Well, she reasoned, I am a big girl and I must learn to stand on my two feet; my father is not going to be around every time I meet my obnoxious brother.

They came into the living room each absorbed in his own thoughts. She would not greet either of them, Tara-Ann decided. If they saw her then it would be different. She thought she would go unnoticed, but Jared walked over to a side table to take up a book. While doing so it fell from his hand, and after picking it up, he noticed Tara-Ann by the window.

"My God, Tara, is really you! Long time no see," shouted Jared, moving across to shake her hand. The handshake became a hug.

Jared's surprised voice reached across to BJ, who was beginning to climb up the stairs. He spun around towards the sound as if his feet were oiled bearings. Instead of standing and staring, he dropped his bag and walked across to her, his serious look turning into hateful intensity. "What are you doing here?" he asked, advancing towards her.

"This is where my father lives," answered Tara-Ann, standing where she was and trying not to feel intimidated by BJ.

"That may be so, but you are not to come here," he said, trying to scorch her with his terrible look.

"BJ, why you talking to your sister like that?" Jared asked, looking at BJ and matching his stare.

"Sister? I don't have any sister! I could never have a thief for a sister," he shouted, looking at Tara-Ann as if daring her to deny the accusation.

"Finding something in somebody's bag does not mean that the person is a thief, especially when other people are around," said Jared defending Tara-Ann, who stood as still as a building looking at BJ. "Somebody could do the same thing to you at school and that would not make you a thief," Jared continued.

"You behave as if you know everything, Solomon. But tell me now, is who put anything in anybody's bag." BJ advanced towards Jared as if he wanted to hit him.

"Why don't you tell me instead," Jared answered. "And anyway, why you so vex, is your money?" Jared asked, looking at BJ with hostility in his eyes.

"Stopsh this at once," shouted a brusque voice from across the room. "You hear mi, boy, stop it at once!"

BJ had to get in the last jab, "You don't belong here. Everything in this house belongs to my family. What else you come to tief now?"

His father who had hobbled over on his crutches made a swipe at him with one and fell to the floor. Tara-Ann,

Jared and Juline, who had come down the stairs and had stood listening to the tirade without interrupting, scrambled to help him up. BJ stood askance as if his father's fall had nothing to do with him. He looked at him disdainfully like a piece of discarded rag, old and filthy.

As soon as he was settled safely back in his chair, he looked straight at BJ and told him, "You havest nothing in herest morest than anyone else. Whatever I havest belongst to all my children not you alone! Don't ever tellst any of my girlst that you arest my heir, when you are not. You hearst me," said Mr. Bernard, sounding pained and tired.

"But what did she say to BJ for him to say that?" Juline asked, pretending not to have overheard most of the conversation.

"Nothing, Mummy. BJ called her a thief and said she was not welcome here," Jared offered and suffered a crushing look for his trouble.

"Well she did steal her father's money the last time she was here,"Juline reminded everyone, trying to provide a basis for BJ's accusation. "Isn't that so, Tara-Ann? The money was found in yours and your sister's suitcase." She nailed home the point, looking triumphantly at Tara-Ann.

Before Tara-Ann could answer, the harsh honking of the taxi intruded on the conversation. Tara-Ann, glad for the welcome avenue of escape, bid everyone goodbye and rushed out.

Juline was not about to put the argument to sleep. As soon as Tara-Ann was gone she attacked Jared. "I caught a part of the argument, Jared, where you trying to tell BJ that somebody else put the money in Tara and her sister's suitcase. Who else could that be, since only Tara and her sisters, BJ and Betty were here?"

"Mom, could we just leave this sick argument alone?" Jared asked, trying to leave the distasteful subject behind.

"Boy, I ask you a question. Don't tell me what I should leave and not leave!" she thundered, challenging Jared and willing him to speak.

"It was easy to figure out," said Jared, looking squarely at his mother, "Tara and Kai troubled BJ and BJ who has easy access to your room and knew that Daddy always leave things lying around, went in there, saw the money and put it in the girl's suitcase to get back at them. Note that there was none in Meisha's suitcase, because he had no quarrel with her." When he had finished, his mother stood staring at him as if she didn't know him. It was not often that Juline's tongue got stuck in her mouth and Jared knew that he was in trouble, but he did not envisage the type of trouble.

Awakening from the shock, Juline stepped forward and struck Jared a resounding slap across his face. Bernard gasped and swore, BJ chuckled, but Jared just stood looking at her and then placed his hand on the affected area and winced.

"Don't you ever do that again as long as you live in this house. Don't tell any lie on BJ and take up for other people, you wretched liad." She spoke slowly, enunciating every word and seemed ready to strike Jared again.

Bernard whose only reaction was the gasping and the swearing spoke, "Youst his mother, but I askst, why you boxst the bwoy for telling the truth? I agree withst Jared. I suspectst him for somest time now. This boyst is capable of doingst almost anythingst," he announced, the girls' innocence finally confirmed in his mind.

"Yes, Daddy, you are always against me! You always against me in everything," BJ said, wheeling to face his father and looking wickedly at him.

"The boy is right," Juline joined in. "Imagine you join with Jared against BJ. So all along the two of you plotting gainst BJ, treating him like the outside pickney, you tink I don't notice it. You tink so." Juline was really riled. Jared had become enemy number one. Anyone who was against BJ was an enemy, but her own son! BJ's own brother, unthinkable!

"Well, Mother, from this day on you will not have any opposition in your house! BJ will live in peace and continue to fill your eyes and your heart. The problem, the mistake, me! will never be around to remind you of your past or to take anything that belongs to BJ! After all, it is my fault to arrive in this world and mess up your life. I will never be a bother again!" Jared walked away and started up the stairs.

"Boy, who are you talking to? Who you tink you talking to? Come back here this minute and apologize to me. What a day I live to see! This boy that I try to give so much and make so much sacrifice for turning on me. You come back here this minute."

Jared continued up the stairs without even a backward glance. There was bumping and thumping coming from his room, but Juline did not go to see what it was. She went into the den with BJ and hugged and soothed him as if he were a baby; telling him that one day his father and brother would see how wrong they were and apologize to both of them. She affirmed that she would never leave him or turn against him but would do anything for him.

About an hour later, a motor vehicle stopped outside the gate and Jared came down the stairs dragging a suitcase. He placed it on the verandah and started up the stairs again. His stepfather's voice stopped him. "Wherest you goingst, Jared? Wherest?"

"Sir, it is best that I leave this house. I am not wanted here," Jared answered, feeling sorry for the man who had only showed him kindness. He would do anything to help his stepfather but at that moment he had to leave.

He went back upstairs and came down again with another suitcase. His mother came out of the den and watched him. BJ had a smug smile on his face in comparison to his mother's snarling scowl. She could not believe her eyes. "Where do you think you are going? Put back your things upstairs," she commanded, but Jared did not respond; it was as if she had not spoken.

He made two more trips and with the last one he stopped beside his stepfather. "Dad, I thank you for everything. I will not forget you. I will see you some time soon."

As he was going through the door his mother's voice followed him, "I hope you will never come running back or ask me for anything again. I hope you will find your own money for university and everything else."

"God will help me," he said and went through the door.

BJ who rarely displayed any form of emotion, especially positive ones, hugged his mother and told her not to worry as they would be all better off.

Later that evening, Bernard's father and brother who partnered with him came to visit. Bernard had asked them there, because he felt propelled to ask their assistance in certain family matters, based on the happenings of the afternoon. They had a private discussion in hushed tones. His brother made notes and altered it more than once. Juline was not invited to the meeting. One time when she ventured close by, they all looked at her as if she was intruding, and the conversation petered off. It started up again as soon as she was safely out of the room.

The following day they both came to pick up Bernard. Juline was surprised because she thought that he had a doctor's appointment she was not aware of. When she asked why she wasn't told about his going out, he told her it had not really been planned. She was even more surprised when she got ready to go with them to be told that it was not necessary, they would get along without her for the outing. Juline was displeased; she knew that something was going on, with the clandestine meeting yesterday and then this trip without her. Let them go ahead, she mused, I have an urgent secret meeting myself. I will not be outdone. She sat down and started to plan her next move, then she too went out.

CHAPTER 11

JULINE ACTS

Juline was almost sorry she had come. Her friend had not told her that the place was so far and remote and the road a mere bridle track filled with sharp stones, numerous puddles and green mossy areas at the sides. The lofty dignified trees soared towards the sky, arresting the sun's glare which fought bravely, but was only able to peep through the leaves weakly. As a result, the road was in semi-darkness as if dark clouds were hovering threateningly overhead.

Juline glanced surreptitiously over her shoulders; clutching her handbag as she did so, fearful that at any moment an animal or someone would spring out of the bushes, which were dwarfed by the trees and attack her. That would be terrible because she could die out here in this bush in Clarendon and no one would find her or know who she was. They would probably take her for one of the peasants from the area especially as she was dressed as one.

Juline was dressed in a worn floral dress, with matching scarf. If there were any bees lurking nearby; they would certainly capitalize on the opportunity to drag her off and extract what nectar they could from her. The scarf covered most of her face, as she did not want to be identified. She wore no makeup and surprisingly her face felt scrubbed and clean. A pair of Jared's old sneakers completed her wardrobe. She presented a pathetic picture, a far cry from the sophisticated, Juline. The only thing that would belie the peasant's garb was the amount of money in her bag. She had no idea how much the man was going to charge so she walked with quite a bit of cash.

Juline was feeling tired. She was not accustomed to walking so far so to her it seemed like miles into the frontier. Her feet hurt and her armpits were soaked despite the absence of the sun's anger. The scarf was also soaked; if she had on makeup it would be rivulets by then. She was ready to sit down by the roadside when the sound of drums beckoned her. She summoned her strength and walked on, fear of the unknown almost crumpling her feet. She screamed lightly when a voice spoke out of nowhere, "Where you going lady?"

She spun around in the direction of the voice but saw no one. The place already had an uncanny atmosphere and the hidden voice only added to it. While she was contemplating running towards the sound of the drums, a tall, bronze man stepped in a lithe manner from the trees. Juline felt as if she were an English Redcoat soldier who had invaded Maroon territory. The bearing, stealthiness and race were present, missing were the leaf covering and the arrow or musket.

"Lady you come to see somebody?" the man asked, standing in front of Juline. The man's scarred face and hand frightened Juline and she stepped back trying to gather her courage.

"A come to see Father Barracks," said Juline, assuming the new voice and language she was told to adopt. Her advisor had warned her that she should appear to be poor as ever or else she would have to pay quite a bit of money for the service.

"Well follow me an' I wi si if him can look bout you," the man offered, leading Juline towards the sound of the drum.

He took her to a house in the middle of a clearing. It was not very big but a reasonable size as country dwellings went. It was painted in red and blue and had many plants around it. Juline had never seen some of these plants before but she guessed at their use and cringed. There were large red flags flying happily in the slight wind. The man led her to the back of the house to a shed and told her to sit. Juline told him it was alright when she looked at the makeshift wooden bench, which was really a long piece of slab nailed between two other vertical pieces of board of the same thickness. It looked dirty and rough and Juline turned her head away in disgust, but as the minutes passed she grew so tired that she had to sit. Her only consolation was that when she got home she would immediately throw everything she was wearing into the garbage and soak her skin for hours. She looked around her and spotted a few houses some distance away. They were all guarded by majestic trees reaching to the heavens. Her ears briefly detected the feeble sounds of a power saw probably being used for the felling of trees. There were some out-buildings closer to her which housed chickens, rabbits and guinea pigs. In a cage nearby there was a strange collection of birds – parrots, an owl and some other brown and black birds of unknown identity.

Juline wondered if she were the only customer. After looking around she saw a couple dressed in black and brown sitting close to some shrubs which grew inside the shed. Their heads were bowed as if they were praying or maybe Juline thought they were trying to avoid detection just as she was. Soon, a lady dressed in white, with a red head wrap came out and ushered the couple inside the house. She did some dips and twirls and chanted some strange words as she danced around them and then behind them. The drum hastened its beat to match her movements. Juline would have laughed if she had been watching them from the safety of her home; but being part of the situation she just sat, bewildered and tense. While the couple was inside other people came. They all kept their heads bowed and spoke in whispers and nods as if they too were afraid.

The woman came back out and sat beside Juline. She was afraid to look at her but grew a little more at ease when she started a conversation. The woman seemed interested in her family, neighbours and life in general. She spoke for a few minutes then left. Juline did not see when the couple left, but after about twenty minutes, another woman wearing a white dress and a similar red head wrap came to get her. She also repeated the dipping and twirling routine to Juline's horror. She hoped she would not touch her while she was performing her antics.

She led her into a small room weakly lit by candles placed around a long table. There was no other light and the candles cast indistinct shadows over the room. Juline thought of fleeing from the ghost-like environment but a voice from the front of the room halted her plan.

"Aha! Whooi! Wat took yuh suh long to come? Aha, yuh wait too long, too long! Aha it almost too late!" the voice rebuked. "Cum forward lady an' let mi see if mi can still help, aha!"

Juline wondered what on earth she was almost too late for. Did this man with the voice like the drum really know what he was saying?

"Cum forward up to the front, aha!" the voice invited. "Cum forward and deal wid di enemy, the direct born of Satan, aha."

Juline felt her way to the front and was soon assisted by a light; which was turned on suddenly at the head of the table. It revealed a mud complexioned, ageless man with a horse-shoe scar in the middle of his forehead. Pock marks created potholes on his face and gave him a scary look. Juline did not really want to stare but could not tear her eyes away.

"Aha, sit down lady rite over there so," he instructed beckoning to a chair upholstered in red. Juline wondered why everything had to be red; the man was wearing a red turban straight out of the Arabian Nights and a long sleeve red and white outfit which she suspected to be a gown.

She sat down gingerly and faced Father Barracks. Now that she was there she did not know how to begin. She did not want to bare her emotions before a stranger, but when she thought of her son, she decided to do it. She cleared her throat and squeezed her fingers under the table and opened her mouth to begin but Father cut in.

"Aha, a know yuh problem but tell it to Father, who you need protection from?" His voice sounded like the strong bellow of a bull and it caused Juline to jump.

"Father a have dis problem, you si. Mi husband don't love mi again an' him worse don't like our legally born son anymore," she said in a rush, glad to have started.

"Aha, somebody tun him mind from the two a yuh. Somebody tun him mind a tell you, aha, aha!"

"Father, you know you rite," Juline blurted out, amazed at the fact that the Father was thinking the same thing she had been thinking all along.

"Aha, Father know it! Father read it up long before yuh come, aha, long before yuh come! Know it an' see it, di angel of the lord show it to mi!" He shouted out to her, emphasizing each word as if he were delivering hammer blows.

"Father, him against us bad, him seem to like him outside pickney dem more than him one boy. Him always fight gainst the bwoy in everything, everything! An' as for me, him don't really love me like a wife again. Me tell you Father, him mind gone from me an' the bwoy." Juline blurted out the information in a spate of words, as if they were pushing against her mouth and she had to free them.

"Aha, yes, the girl dem! The girl dem tun him mind gainst you! Aha, tun him mind gainst you!" he said, bending his head close to Juline's face to allow the information to sink in.

Juline was becoming more and more awed. She had not mentioned the girls yet the Father knew about them! He really was knowledgeable! He must be hearing from God! It was a good thing she had come. "Yes Father, him have three outside girls an' him seem to be paying them more mind than his one lawful bwoy pickney. Nex ting we know something happen to him an' my bwoy nuh get nutten! Father a need you to fix dat!" She placed her hands on the rough table in a pleading manner, exposing her expensive wedding band which she had forgotten to remove.

Father looked at the ring and then at Juline. "Yes, ah going to fix everything. A will fix everything but you have to pay! It will cost you, aha!" he bellowed.

"I am not a rich woman an' a can't afford much, a will pay you wat a have because I need mi life to come back right." Juline said vehemently, as if stressing her wish would help to accomplish it.

Father got up and went into an inner room. Juline wondered what he was doing inside. While he was gone, she took the time to look around her. The small room had only one small window which was close to the ceiling. It was curtainless and half shut and aided the darkness in the room. The candles were really the only source of light. The room contained no other piece of furniture but the table and the three chairs around it. Juline was expecting to see a crystal ball and huge cauldrons boiling, but concluded that all of those must be in the room which Father had gone into.

He came back in fifteen minutes with a number of phials in his hands. "Aha, lady lissen to me carefully, dis bottle with the red cover is for you husband. Aha, put one cover full into him drink until it is finished. An' this one with the blue cover, aha, mus' mix up wid him food. Aha, then this big one with the yellow top mus' use to bathe the bwoy ebry morning, him mus' wear this chain roun' him neck an' him mus' not take it off. It will kip off trouble off a him. Aha, mind you, him mus' always wear it." He handed Juline a chain with a pendant that had some strange markings on it. Juline could not make out any of the symbols, but did not allow that to bother her. Anything that Father gave her must be important. He was already explaining them so there was no reason to question him further. Father continued, "Now you, you mus' always wear something red whether under clothes or ordinary clothes, aha, that will protect you from even Satan himself. Sprinkle you clothes with dis powder," he said, handing her a plastic container of powder. "But one ting though wen it finish you gwine have to come back for more aha, or a can get somebody to deliver it to you fi a price whichever you choose."

"A will mek arrangement for you to deliver it, Father," Juline quickly put in. She had no intention of making this trip again unless it was absolutely necessary. She asked for a piece of paper and then wrote an address and asked him for a telephone number. She chose a secret place some distance from her home and workplace. It would never do for anyone she knew to see her meeting with unsavoury characters.

"Now for the girl dem, you need to get dem picture and put dem into dis jar here. Always keep the jar shut and dat will tek care a dat."

Father finally completed all the instruction and Juline was free to go. The same tall, bronze man accompanied her all the way to the main road; where she took a taxi that carried her back to her friend's house and her SUV. While she changed out of the despicable peasant clothing, she thought about the amount of money this whole thing had cost her, twenty five thousand dollars! Twenty five thousand dollars all for BJ. She consoled herself that it was a small price to pay for her son's safety and future. She had done it all for her son so that he would not be left out. He deserved to have his father's love and whatever his father had. Going to an obeah man was not exactly her way, but if that was what it took for her son to triumph and gain all that was legally his, then she would do it again and again.

CHAPTER 12

NIGHT RIDE

It was ten o'clock and BJ was already late for his date. Already he had received five calls from his friends who were waiting for him to pick them up. When they rang the sixth time he completely ignored it. Let them wait, he had already told them he was coming, what more did they expect him to do. He manoeuvred the SUV through the busy night traffic, flew through a red light and then headed out on a less busy street. When he had gone about two miles into a quiet residential area, he stopped at a crossroad and shut off the engine. In about a minute he heard footsteps approaching, he opened the door of the SUV and admitted five of his friends, three girls and two boys, all grade eleven students like himself.

"Yute, you took a long time to come, eh," said Tenishay, who was BJ's closest girlfriend. She was dressed in a pink sleeveless summer dress, with matching long leg tights and pink flat shoes decked with silver sequins. The headband was of the same shade and was also covered with sequins. The other two girls, Reniesha and Larnette were in similar pink outfits.

"Remember I had to wait until my parents fell asleep," BJ reminded them without displaying any sympathy for being late. "An' then you keep calling me for them to suspect something," he reprimanded.

"But, BJ, don't you say the vehicle covered and it wouldn't be a problem," Brandon reminded him.

"Yes, but remember say is only a learner's me have so it would cause whole heap a argument about me driving out late at night by myself; so I have to wait until them fall asleep," he answered shortly, giving a hint that he did not like being questioned.

Brandon did not get the hint from the tone of voice and continued, "Bwoy, your parents go to bed early eh, after nine o'clock! My parents dem stay up until after eleven, twelve sometimes," Brandon said surprised.

"So how did you get out?" Larnette asked, turning around to look at Brandon.

"I pretended to be ill an' then turn off the light and went to bed. I even locked my room door. Then after that I just snucked out the window and pushed it out from out-side; easy, easy," boasted Brandon.

"Well good for you, "BJ snapped. "You only had your-self to get out of the house. I had myself and the vehicle!" he said it with such finality that all the others except Brandon knew to leave the subject alone.

"Well, BJ, you always get to have your way so I wasn't really worried about you not coming. And you girls it was easy as eating," Brandon said.

"Ours was easier than eating, I invited my friends to spend the weekend, cause I know my mother is on the night shift at the hospital for the rest of the week, so easy, easy," supplied Tenishay.

"Could we just get the hell to the party and stop chatting garbage," BJ snapped. His face was red and expressionless as he concentrated on the road.

Brandon took one look at BJ's face and fell silent. He had been friends with BJ long enough to know what that particular expression meant. Sometimes he wished that he could get out of BJ's company. He was alright in some ways as good friends went but there were times when he became deadly intense about small things. He sometimes got the impression that BJ was just ticking, biding his time, waiting to erupt into violence or do something mean. He hoped he would not be the one to be in the middle of the explosion, he hoped that none of the shrapnel of the bomb would hit him. Watching his handsome face now, he could feel the mood relaxing, slowly receding like waves after a storm.

They soon got to the party hosted by one of their grade eleven friends who 'borrowed' the house from a friend who had gone abroad. The party was well on its way when they got there. There were no adult chaperones, and except for the young men who were responsible for playing the music there were only teenagers present. BJ looked around carefully and noted that many of them were not from his school and must be friends of the host. Somebody had provided food from the money they had contributed. There were many different types of sandwiches, fried chicken, fruit cocktail, different types of dessert and other delicacies available. There were also a variety of drinks available which ranged from ordinary soft drink to Smirnoff vodka.

BJ helped himself to a few sandwiches and fruit cocktail and then sat outside with Tenishay talking. His other companions were inside either eating or drinking or dancing to the throbbing, screaming music. BJ spoke a little to Tenishay. He was a good conversationalist at times but he seemed to be somewhat distracted that night. Tenishay wanted to dance but BJ told her he was not interested in dancing at that moment. She left him alone and went in search of fun.

When she was gone BJ's phone rang. He scrutinized the number and recognized it as his paternal grandfather and decided not to answer it. He wondered why he should be calling him at that hour or even calling him at all. The phone rang six more times and then BJ decided to answer it. He went as far away from the music as he could so that his grandfather would not hear it.

"Hello, good night," he answered irritably, hoping that his grandfather would say what he had to and get off his phone.

"BJ, where are you? I have been calling and calling the house since minutes to ten and no one has answered.

Where is your mother and father and why are you playing the music so loud in your room at this time of the night? No wonder you can't hear the phone!" his grandfather said.

"Mummy and daddy are asleep. They went to bed early. I went to sleep too, but I woke up afterwards and start listening to some music so that's why I didn't hear the phone," he rattled off the information quickly, hoping to get rid of his grandfather's interfering voice.

"Well since it is so late don't bother to wake them up. I will come and see them tomorrow," he said. "Oh and turn down the music, it's too late to be playing music so loud." He then hung up.

BJ smiled to himself, so he had fooled his grandfather! He thought he was playing music indeed! What a laugh! He somehow felt in a better mood and went in search of his friends. He always felt good when he got the better of someone else. He found Tenishay dancing with Brandon and demanded her. She left Brandon and danced with BJ, then declared she was tired. They went outside to sit down, but not before they had taken two bottles of beer. BJ was not sure that Tenishay should be drinking so he cautioned her, "I don't think as a girl you should be drinking so much strong drink. Put back one!" he ordered.

"No," said Tenishay, "I can hold my liquor just as well as any man," she defended her decision.

"Shay, don't bother with it. What if you mother find out?" BJ asked.

"Well, she knows that I tek a one drink sometimes so it wouldn't be anything," she said, sitting and starting on one of the drink.

Not to be outdone in an argument, BJ moved over and took one of the drink from her before she realized what he was doing.

"Now BJ, what did you do that for?" Tenishay asked, annoyed at BJ's action. She looked at him in an unkind manner.

"You are not to have so much strong drink, you are a girl," BJ emphasized, opening the drink and pouring it on the ground.

"Okay, BJ, what if I did that with yours?" Tenishay asked, peeved.

"No, you don't," said BJ in an irritated tone. Just like when they were coming to the dance and he had put an abrupt end to the argument, his tone of voice reflected the same impatience and annoyance.

"You always love to get the last word," Tenishay commented, vexed. "You…"

Her words were cut short by shouts of, "Police! Police! Police! The lookout say police a come."

BJ looked at his watch; it was two-thirty. He had no idea it was so late. He quickly called everyone, and they jumped into the vehicle, except Brandon. He came running a bit unsteadily just as BJ was moving off.

"BJ, were you really going to leave me?" he asked, surprise in his voice.

"You think I want police to catch me here?" he fired back, moving down the driveway.

"I wouldn't have done that to you," Brandon replied, angry at BJ's word. "I thought we were supposed to be friends," Brandon added sulking.

"Friend or no friend, I don't want no harassment from any police, an' anyway I can avoid that, I am going to avoid it. So whether you did come or you don't come is so. I gone!" he shouted, screeching through the gate.

Brandon did not answer; he simply closed his eyes and thought somehow I must get out of BJ's company! The idea hit him that they were almost at the end of grade eleven, and if he qualified for sixth form, he would go to another school or better yet he would try and get his parents to send him abroad to study and live with one of his relatives. He smiled at the idea. Why didn't he think of it before?

They left the community and headed out on the main road. An uneasy silence smothered the vehicle. They all knew that BJ was driving too fast, but no one said anything because they didn't want to start the argument again. As they headed down the long straight road they heard the police siren screaming somewhere behind them. At first they were not certain if they were being chased or not, but after a few minutes they realized that they were the target. BJ accelerated with the intention to outwit the police.

"BJ, I think it is better to pull over and take the ticket instead of getting us all killed!" Reneisha shouted, frightened as the scenery rushed towards them, set on collision course.

"Reneisha is right, BJ. Slow down and pull over before you kill us!" Phillip said. He rarely spoke unless it was necessary and he had spoken because he knew their lives were threatened.

BJ did not answer; instead he drove faster. The girls started to scream along with the police siren. As they rounded a corner, the door on Brandon's side swung wide open and he fell outside.

"Dear God, Brandon drop out! Him drop out!" Larnette bawled, covering her face.

"Jesus Christ him mus' dead!" Phillip shouted. "BJ slow down and stop! Jesus Christ! Let we help him quick before something run over him! BJ stop!" Phillip was almost hysterical; tears were rushing down his face.

BJ shouted back, "You tink I going to any jail because of any-one? You think so! Shut the hell up and let me concentrate," he shouted back angrily still driving fast.

"But BJ, Brandon might be dead for all we know! BJ stop and let us help him even if the police lock us up," Tenishay pleaded, touching BJ on the shoulder. He shrugged off her hand and continued to drive. Obviously he had said all he was going to say and that was it.

Everyone except BJ was crying. Phillip kept hitting his head on the seat in front of him, and then he blurted out: "Let me out BJ! Let me out! Let me out right now before I grab the steering wheel out of your hand and turn over the wretched SUV! Let me out!" he started getting up, bent on carrying out his threat.

BJ glanced around at Phillip and saw naked anger on his face. He knew that Phillip was going to make good his threat so he pulled over. Not only did Phillip jump out but also the three girls. They would walk all the way back if it took all night to look for Brandon. They did not care anymore what would happen to them. The horror of what had happened numbed them of any thought of their own welfare.

BJ looked at the vehicle emptying out behind him and said unfeelingly, "What good do you think you can do by going back there? By the time you get back there whatever is to happen will happen."

"Stay if you want to, you obnoxious vermin!" said Phillip, walking off.

At the same time, a vehicle swooped down and stopped beside them. BJ tried to close the SUV doors and start up the vehicle, but the vehicle went in front of him and blocked the way. Defeated, BJ sat in the vehicle and closed the door. The police officer ordered him out but he sat staring at them as if he had a hearing defect. One of the police officers yanked open the back door, pointed a gun at BJ and ordered him out.

In the light from the police vehicle, BJ made out his companions huddled together in a group and flanked by two police officers. The girls were crying, and Phillip started blubbering, "Can we go and look for Brandon? Did you see him by the road?"

"Who is Brandon?" asked one police officer.

"He was in the SUV with us and he fell out!" Phillip cried. "Please Sir, is he okay?"

"So you are the wicked ones whose friend fell out of a vehicle and you keep driving? You are the wickedest brutes I've ever come across!" explained one of the officers standing by the group. "Generation of vipers and murderers!" he added, expressing his disgust and utter disbelief.

"It wasn't us, Sir. We tried to get BJ to stop but he wouldn't!" said Tenishay.

"He just wouldn't no matter what we said," said Phillip sniffing loudly. "Sir, could you tell us what happen to Brandon? We didn't mean for any of this to happen. It was all an accident," he begged, hoping that the officer would just set his mind at ease.

"Where were you coming from?" said the officer, postponing a response to Phillip's question.

No one answered and another officer asked, "Is it di big dance which disturb the people dem community?"

Still no one answered. The officers herded them into the two vehicles and drove them to the police station. On the way Phillip begged again to be told of Brandon's condition. "He is in the hospital, and I think he will live," he answered shortly, not divulging any other information.

The group was relieved and would have liked more information but dared not ask for any details, added to the worry about Brandon; they now started to fret about their fate. What would the officers do to them, and how would their parents react to what they had done? They knew their parents would never trust them again; especially because of their deception. They were even more afraid of what Brandon's parents would say and think about the manner in which he had been treated by BJ.

Once they reached the police station, the officers took their parents' telephone numbers and called them. There was no response from BJ's home. The officers rang both land lines and cellular phones without success. BJ maintained that he had left them sleeping at home. Eventually, they called his uncle, who partnered in the motor vehicle business with his father. Before he went to the station, he asked another brother to go and check on his brother and his wife.

When he got to the station it was about four thirty a.m. and the other parents were almost ready to leave. He did not greet BJ or try to find out if he was alright. To say he was indignant was an understatement. "Who gave you permission to leave the house?" he roared at BJ. Before he could answer he thundered at him, "And who told you to take Bernard's vehicle? You don't even have a driver's licence."

"That's exactly it," said one of the police officers in agreement. "He's under age for driving. He was driving a vehicle without the owner's consent even though it belongs to his father. He was speeding, almost one hundred and sixty kilometres per hour, and the worst evil that I have ever seen." Here he paused not because he was out of breath, but because he was trying to understand or rationalize the evil in his mind. "His friend fell out of the vehicle, and he drove away without stopping, not caring whether his friend was dead or not! Beat that! You beat that!" He stood up and banged the table as if he expected an answer from it or expected BJ's uncle to provide a more horrifying story.

BJ's uncle looked at him without saying a word. In his mind he knew that the boy was trouble. He had told his brother before his accident to send him to a boarding school; to teach him self reliance and get him out of the mother's grasp, so that she would stop spoiling him. He did not listen to him and he was angry that he was the one to represent BJ in his disgrace. He really didn't want to have anything to do with Juline and her boys. His brother had been rendered a near handicapped man, walking like a see-saw, talking with a lisp and look at his face! He was sure one of them was responsible for the accident! Bernard had said when he got out of the SUV that night the brakes were holding okay, but by early morning it had malfunctioned. The way he saw it, one or all three were responsible for his brother's accident and one day he would find out who it was and why he, she, or they wanted him dead!

"What you going to do with him?" BJ's uncle asked nonchalantly in a tone showing that he didn't really care.

"They are all to report here tomorrow morning, well it's already morning, by ten with the parents and then we will contact the schools an' take it from there."

Before they left the station, BJ's uncle's phone rang. He answered it, listened to the speaker on the other end and then hung up. He did not say one word to BJ as they walked out, neither did he utter one word as he drove home in his SUV. His brother's SUV was left at the station to be collected in the morning.

As he drove, BJ's uncle reflected on a conversation he had had three years before with his brother.

"BJ and Juline want us to go to England for the summer. Some of BJ's friends have been there and he wants to go too." Bernard told his brother one day as they sat at lunch at the business place.

"Do you want to go to England?" Kenton asked.

"Not really," Bernard said, "Is really BJ who wants to go."

"Why you always doing everything that boy ask you to do?" Kenton questioned, turning to his brother.

"Well is the only son I have, and I always try my best to make him happy," Bernard responded, wondering why his brother had made that observation.

"If you ask me, you spoiling that boy too much. The type of things you get for him – swimming pool, horse, fancy unnecessary games you name them. You must let the boy wait and earn some of these things. If you give him everything him not going to turn out good! He will take it for granted, that he must have everything him want in this life as soon as him want it, without working for it." Kenton said, looking meaningfully at his brother. He didn't mean to be rude; but he had been listening to Bernard carry on about BJ and all the things that Juline said he was to get for him.

Bernard looked at his brother in a strange way, as if he could not believe that was the opinion that his brother had of him and how he conducted things. He knew he was indulgent, but he never really thought of it as spoiling the boy. "You know I never really look at it that way before. I know his mother like me to treat him special and make him feel happy; but I really never think it was spoiling him and leading him to wrong assumptions."

"I suggest that you consider it. Fail to give him something that him ask for one of the time and note the reaction and see if what I just said make any sense," he advised.

Not long after Bernard had told him that what he said made much sense, but it seemed that his advice had come a little too late.

When they arrived home, BJ told his uncle to leave him at the gate. His uncle took one look at him and drove inside. When they got to the verandah, he saw his grandfather and another of his uncle sitting outside. BJ missed a step and almost fell, but he regained his composure and continued to the door.

"Do you have the keys, BJ?" his uncle Kenton asked, glaring at him.

"No, I don't," he answered shortly.

"How did you get out?" asked his grandfather. "We have been calling and trying to get in but no one is answering," he said anxiously. "What do you mean you don't have the keys, boy?"

"I do not have the keys," BJ said calmly, not looking at anyone.

"I will use mine," said his uncle Kenton. "Ever since Bernard had the accident, he gave me one in case of emergency and is a good thing, because something strange is happening here." He turned and looked at BJ meaningfully then added, "As a matter of fact, you will not enter through this door, go in the way you came out."

BJ looked at his uncle with eyes of sharpened swords, but did not argue. His uncle placed himself in front of the door as soon as he had allowed his father and brother to go in. He stood and watched as BJ pushed open one of the living room windows and jumped through.

"There's only one kind of person that I know who walk through windows and so easily like an expert," declared his uncle, shaking his head disgustingly. "You…" his words were suspended by a shout from his father.

"Kenton come here quickly!" the voice sounded worried and frightened.

Kenton rushed to his father's side. Bernard was sitting in his massage chair, seemingly fast asleep, while Juline was lying in the settee. They were not responding to the calls and shakes.

BJ's uncle, Radcliffe, who had not spoken so far, screamed out, "Come here, bwoy, tell me what you do to you parents? Tell me, bwoy, what you do to you parents?" He was shaking like jelly and his lips were twitching furiously.

"They are breathing Radcliffe, Daddy, but they not waking up at all! Something happen to them," Kenton shouted.

All three tried to wake them but they did not respond. BJ stood close to his mother and looked at her nervously and anxiously. He did not even glance in his father's direction.

"Call the ambulance and the police!" shouted Kenton's father to his two sons. "Call them quickly and when you finish call Juline mother!" He went from one to the other still trying to shake them awake. He gave up after the calls were made and as he sat awaiting the ambulance he said to BJ, "You better tell me what happen here." His voice was very cold and controlled.

"I don't know, I left them here asleep," he said, keeping to the story he had given to his friends and the police.

"Yes, but how did they conveniently fall asleep just before you left? How did you manage to put them to sleep? They just did not fall asleep like that?" he accused, hoping to break down the boy.

"What do you mean, what did I give them? I am not the cook around here! I am not the one who feed them?" he answered rudely.

"Yes, but you were the only one in the house. Betty leave long long time an' gone bout her business. I call your father up to eight o'clock and he was awake and fine! So anything that happen must happen after I call!"

"I believe the bwoy give them something to put them to sleep so that he could tief out and tief the SUV without any problem!" said Radcliffe. "I think that is exactly what happen!" He jumped up triumphant that he had solved the mystery.

"You know that sound quite possible. I believe that is what happen. Him dose them so that he could get out! What a hell, wretched bwoy! A wonder how my brother manage to get a wretch like this!" He circled BJ, like a wild cat ready to tear him apart, but he did not touch him and BJ did not move. He only stood looking at his uncle, frozen and unmoved.

The ambulance came and took BJ's parents to the hospital. The doctors found that they had ingested a number of sleeping pills, which had knocked them out completely because of the large dosage. Radcliffe had been right but BJ denied being the one who gave them the pills. Betty when questioned denied giving them anything. She was aghast at the idea, that anyone could even think of her hurting a family that had always been kind to her. Apart from BJ, who acted up sometimes, she had never really had any problems with them, she told their families and the police. She packed up whatever she had at the Hemmings' house and she did not return.

CHAPTER 13

⁂

THE FAMILY SPEAKS OUT

As soon as Bernard and Juline were released from the hospital, members of both families assembled at the Hemmings' house. There were both grandparents, his uncles Radcliffe and Kenton, his aunts Angina and Kimeral and Jared looking very uncomfortable. They had waited until BJ got home from school in the afternoon. When he arrived and saw them, his already serious face took on an even more dour look. He knew they were not just there to visit his parents but were there hovering, like john crows, waiting anxiously for the kill. He looked at the faces and wished them all dead, even his brother, Jared, what was he doing back in the house? He looked very relaxed and pensive; he could expect no sympathy from that direction. He was not a brother in the real sense as brothers go. Imagine accusing him of treachery in front of the three usurpers. His two uncles and their father thought they were wise and could undo him but let them continue to float in the air; he and his mother would give them a bumpy landing.

He mumbled a forced good afternoon and started up the stairs to his room, but his uncle Kenton's voice stalled him.

"BJ, could you come back here, we need to talk to you." He sounded very serious as if he were not in the mood to brook any argument from BJ.

"I'm tired and I need to lie down for a while," BJ answered, hoping to get away.

"You can lie down all you want to when we are finished here," he returned, giving him a hard look.

"Why can't he lie down first?" his mother said, "He was out all day and must really be tired." She looked from BJ to his uncle, wanting to avert the unpleasantness she saw coming.

"BJ comest herest this minute," his father ordered, fixing Juline a crushing look. "Comest herest right now!"

BJ looked at his father's commanding look and ambled back into the living room, seemingly unconcerned. He stood a little distance away from them and waited for the diatribe to begin. He did not have long to wait.

"Tell me, BJ," his grandfather began, "where did you get the pills that you gave your parents?" He looked straight at BJ waiting for an answer.

"I did not give anybody any pill," he answered shortly, looking straight at his grandfather.

"Come now bwoy, it is time you stop lying! Where did you get those pills?" his uncle Radcliffe asked.

"But Radcliffe, BJ said he did not give us any pills," said Juline, "why you accusing him? He …"

"Juline shutst up or tellst us who putst the pills into our drinkst!" Bernard said angrily.

"Don't you talk to me like that and in front of other people," Juline snapped at him, surprised at his reaction and embarrassed that he had been rude to her in the presence of others.

"Wellst wake upst and getst some senset beforest this boy ruin youst! Wakest up!" he said, his temper rising with each word.

"Juline and Bernard, a think you should try an' not argue so much or we will never get anywhere this day," Juline's mother interjected. She too was annoyed with Juline, but she did not want to expose her feelings in front of others.

"Again I ask you where did you get those pills?" Radcliffe asked, seizing the moment to get the inquisition going again.

"Again I tell you I did not give anybody any pill!" BJ stoutly defended himself.

"Yes you did, just so you could go to the silly dance," his Aunt Kimeral charged, wondering at the stubbornness of the boy. "Who else could have done it? You were the only one here. You need to stop lying!" she added.

"How come everybody come into this house attacking my boy and calling him liad!" Juline exploded. "How come!"

"You know, a really don't believe any of this!" said Juline's father. "A really don't believe you. Give us an explanation for this strange business. You nearly dead but you don't really care! You husband nearly dead but you don't really care! All you care about is saying that is not the boy! Juline a wat wrong wid you?" her father said, looking at his daughter, trying to understand her strange behaviour.

"Juline who put the pills in the drink?" asked Kenton, giving her a scorching look. "You say it's not BJ, it could not have been Betty, so who did? Unless you or Bernard did plan to commit suicide, which I find hard to believe!"

Juline just stared at Kenton as if she had never seen him before. He could have been an apparition; beamed down from another world who understood how to speak English, but was not making sense. When she had recovered enough from his scorching words, she spoke into the still silence which had eyes trying to pierce her, trying to get into her inner being and wrench out her feelings and secrets. She felt that if she remained silent; the eyes might begin to bore through the barrier which she had erected with defiance and trust in her boy. "Believe anything you want to, say anything you want to, do anything you want to! But unless you and the police have evidence about anybody in this house, you can always talk on."

"You really are a ridiculous woman. You running away from facts and reality an' fooling your own self!" Bernard's father said in mock amusement. "And why were you trying to kill yourself an' carry my son with you?" he lashed out, hoping to subdue Juline so that they could get on trying to get the truth out of BJ.

"I really don't think that Juline was trying to kill herself or her husband," Juline's mother remarked. "I don't think she is a murderer, just a mother who protecting her son when she should be correcting him." She turned to Juline and pleaded, "Juline help the bwoy to speak the truth. Help him before it too late. Rudeness, drugs, deception and lying mek sweet recipe for destruction! Destruction that will destroy dis whole family, mark my words!"

"Why everyone think I protecting BJ? Why? I am just saying that he said it's not him! That's all!" Juline tried to explain.

"Well, Juline, again I asking the same question everybody asking, if is not BJ, then who? Pills don't have hands to put themselves into people body! Somebody or something mus' do the putting! Who else was in the house?" Juline's father's face was stark bewilderment as he commented and questioned his daughter.

"All thist ist foolishness Juline," said Bernard. "Don't interruptst against. Sincest you are not willingst to helpst yourst own child. Letst those who meanst him wellst do it. Thatst the best you canst do." His eyes were sharp blades ready to cut her if she persisted in her defence.

BJ's Uncle Radcliffe took up the dropped baton and started the aborted questioning again. "BJ, tell me, who gave you the pills for your parents? Do you realize that you could have killed the two of them with an overdose just like how you almost kill yourself with drugs?" he asked, trying to help BJ see the error of his ways.

"Why you have to remind him about that unfortunate incident?" Juline jumped in, forgetting that Bernard had commanded her to be quiet.

Everyone looked from Juline to Bernard and back again to Juline, wondering why she didn't keep quiet? Why was she so bent on shielding the boy?

"Juline letst me askst youst politely; leave this roomst so thatst we canst reach somewherest! Leavest this roomst! You standing on myst last nerve!" he jumped up and grabbed his stick but Jared stepped in his path.

"Dad, do not get yourself into trouble. Do not hit Mummy even though she might be doing the wrong thing. It is frustrating yes, but don't hit her!" For a moment Bernard stood his ground looking irritatingly at Jared who was almost as tall as he was. Jared, now almost twenty had grown into a striking young man. His broad shoulders and sturdy body were difficult to go unnoticed in any circle. This was complimented by his unassuming very intelligent look. Bernard could tell that behind his unpretentious exterior, there was hurt and pain and smouldering anger at the way he had been treated by his mother. He had borne it well, Bernard concluded, too well. He still called his mother on Mother's Day and at special times to wish her well. Bernard had reached the opinion, that the boy must have inherited his pleasing personality from his father's side. He had met his father a few times and he bore him no ill will for having been involved with Juline, that was before him and he had a right to his son, just as he had a right to his daughters and they to him.

He went back to sit down but held his stick threateningly. Jared positioned himself at his side and stayed there for the duration of the inquisition. He spoke from his seat, "Juline forst the last timest keepst your mouth shutst or leavest us alone. You Hearst me. Leave this thingst alone!" His face looked exhausted and jaded as if he wished to see the end of it all.

"Even if she put herself in again we will just ignore her," Radcliffe declared. "BJ, do you know what they do to murderers in this country?" he asked, looking directly at BJ who was glowering at him. "Do you know that they send them to prison for life? Do you know that they are raped and beaten inside there and that after awhile it is like you are not even a person?" He stressed each word hoping to see some sign of fear on BJ's face but there was none, just the nonchalant, blank stare as if no one had spoken or was even there.

"BJ, it is not an easy place to be at all," his maternal grandfather said, shaking his finger at BJ and putting on a very serious face.

"Why should I be going to prison? Which crime I commit?" BJ asked, turning to look at everyone present, his voice and his eyes declaring innocence.

"Let me tell you what you have done in case yuh suffering from premature senility," Bernard's father said. "And in case you don't know what ah mean, you seem to be getting old and forgetful before time. One, you almost kill yuh parents with sleeping pills just to get out an' have your fun;

two, you take your father SUV without permission an' drive it without a driver's licence; three, you break the speed limit on the road and wickedness heightened, you cause your friend to drop out of the van an' speed away, leaving him to the mercy of ole iron!" He finished the charges and looked around him for support. This he received from loud grunts and the nodding of heads of everyone, except Juline, who placed her left hand akimbo and glared at the wall before her and then at Jared; who stood by impassively just staring at BJ.

BJ did not answer at first; he seemed to be thinking of an appropriate response. His expression remained unchanged; as if the charges were fabricated and totally unrelated to him.

"What do you have to say for yourself," Juline's mother prompted, breaking the silence. "What cause you to do all these things when you know that you father not well already and you mother been through a lot?" She looked at him, signs of worry and confusion appearing on her face. Even though he was bad, she thought, he was still her daughter's child, and whatever happened to him it would affect the whole family. Already people were asking her questions. One neighbour wanted to find out if it was the same boy who had the strange illness some time before who was giving trouble again. She had launched off on a list of evils being done by teenagers and how they were the last generation connected directly to Satan, whose type the world had never seen before and would never see again.

"You need to speak the truth an' make up your mind to do better," his maternal grandfather joined in. "If you don't, you going to end up straight a prison as sure as God mek man. And prison is not a nice place, not a nice place at all. An' every day you would sit down in there remembering how you kill off you parents an' you friend. That is a whole heap a problem for one somebody to carry on him head, whole, whole heap."

"What you need is a good beaten, some of the real old time one, that you parents should have given you a long time ago instead of spoiling you!" his Uncle Kenton declared.

Bernard did not respond to the jab, but kept his eyes averted from his brother's. He stared at nothing in particular to hide his embarrassment at being chided in front of so many persons, especially BJ and Jared. He was a mature man, he thought and despite his disabilities, he still had a voice. He was still performing the role of husband, father and chief bread-winner in his house and it irked him to be publicly chastised, albeit by his family. It was even more searing that they were right! It was certainly one of the most embarrassing moments of his life. He had allowed Juline to hoodwink him with her honeyed tone, using her slogan, "He is your only son".

"We don't even know what the police are going to do with him yet and then there is the matter of the boy who was injured; his parents have not contacted us yet," Kenton said, putting reality right under their noses. "We need to go and see them, but I don't even have the time to. All this foolishness is causing us to lose business. I'm not complaining, but you know how much time this boy has cost us and the company, first when he fed himself white death and now when him decide to test the law."

"And if I sum up the situation right, the school would not mind getting rid of him. Then what will become of him? The police might even sen' him to reform school. Last night, they were suggesting that his parents cannot control him and that the state would do a better job," stated Kenton, painting a picture of total despair. "And the problem is this boy will not admit to anything at all! He does not even look sorry for one minute! We don't seem to be reaching him and Juline, you not making it easy for us," declared Radcliffe, looking accusingly at Juline, who stared straight in front of her as if no one had spoken. For once her tongue was in-active, stilled either by Radcliffe's words or her husband's demand to keep still.

"Well," said Juline's mother, "BJ, you are in real trouble an' you need to change you ways. You see that yuh poor father is not one hundred percent an' yet you continue to give him trouble. You need to change yuh ways an' settle down, so that something good can come of you. Think 'bout how yuh nearly did kill off three people in one night! My skin quake to even think of it. Jesus Christ!" There were grunts of assent all around except from Juline and BJ. Bernard's embarrassment was acute, he felt like a fly in front of his family and in-laws. He had been brought low, rendered almost useless. The sleeping pills had affected his already fragile structure and he was feeling weak and disoriented. His head felt as if someone had loaded bags of cement on it and he was tottering under the weight. He closed his eyes and wished he had died when he had the accident. They were some things worse than death. He felt he must look like a pathetic figure to his wife, slurred speech, see-saw walk and patched face. He knew that she had been vain about his good looks and had always wanted to be in his company in his pre-accident days, but now he felt she only tolerated him and remained with him, only because criticisms from family and friends would condemn her. He wished that she would go away and take the boy with her instead of torturing him, with her bouts of mood swings which ranged from fussing around him and his food, to bouts of sullenness especially when he decried any of BJ's negative attitudes. He put his head in his hands and drove back the tears of pity which were fighting to embarrass him.

He looked up when he heard shouts of, "Boy come back here, we talking to you!" and "How could you?" He followed the direction of their voices and he saw BJ almost at the top of the stairs. When he got to his room, he went in and slammed the door which protested so loudly that the crockery in the breakfront joined in.

"Well God hear me!" said Juline's mother. "God hear me! I wash my hands and wipe dem off this bwoy! I shake the dust off mi shoes from this bwoy!" With that, she picked up her bag and called those who had accompanied her.

151

She left without saying goodbye to anyone, not even her daughter, who stared both at her and the stairs in a questioning manner.

CHAPTER 14

THE POLICE INTERVENE

The following day the police paid BJ a visit at school. When the principal sent to his class to get him, he hissed his teeth and offered to pay a boy to tell him he had not seen him.

"Ah will give you two bills to tell him you didn't see me," he said, reaching into his pocket for the money.

The boy watched as he fumbled through a number of denominations, thousands, five hundreds and hundreds before extracting the two hundred dollars. His eyes opened wide and the tempter whispered in his ears but he resisted. "No way, you tink you can buy me? You tink I want to get into trouble over one little two hundred dollar?" he asked, stepping away from BJ.

"Jus' cool no man, take five then and tell him that you no se mi," he cajoled, as he walked up to the boy and pushed the money into his face.

"My yute, you deaf or what? Me want to graduate from this place with a clean sheet. I don't want no rap sheet like yours. Keep yuh money!" With that, he walked off down the stairs without looking back.

BJ made a serious face at him; he did not call to him again, but made a mental note of the refusal. He shook his head and muttered, "You dis, we will see my boss." With that, he went into his classroom, picked up his bag and competed with the snail for slowness as he made his way to the office.

He was met outside by two highly irritated policemen; their patience had ebbed away with the long wait. They glared at him and one asked, "You related to worm or what? Look how long we sit here waiting for you. Come along, you parents waiting for you at the station."

BJ made no indication that he had heard. He simply ambled out in front of them; forcing them to walk as if they were going off duty. By the time they had got to the car park, a large number of students and teachers had gathered to watch the procession. They were curious to know what he had done. One boy said he had heard that he had almost killed Brandon, his best friend. In a little while, different variations of the story had spread through the crowd like a popular DJ song. BJ did not glance at the crowd not even once, they may not have existed at all.

When they got to the station his parents were there. BJ's father looked at him in disdain while his mother greeted him with apparent concern. "Hello son, we will soon get to go home so you can get something to eat and get some rest."

Everybody looked at her without commenting. The look was not lost on her and she kept quiet.

A third officer joined the first two and the meeting commenced. "Well," said the newcomer, "we are all aware of the particulars of this case so we need not revisit them; question is, what do we do with this young man, seeing that he is underage? Should we send him off to reform school; seeing that his parents seem not to be able to manage him..."

"That's not true!" Juline interjected. "How many times has he ever been brought to you?"

"Miss, could you allow me to finish my statement?" the officer said. "Good, let me continue. As I was saying, you parents do not seem to be able to curb this young man, so wouldn't it be best if we send him where he will be forced to listen. He definitely needs..."

"Sir, he does not need that kind of rough life. My son is not accustomed to living with all kind of people and living the life of a prisoner." Juline chipped in, raw horror pouring out of her eyes at the thought of her beloved being taken away to endure such an existence as reform school.

"Miss, I do not like to be interrupted while I am speaking, your turn will come. Do not do it again, I will not have it!" He was trying hard to remain calm and be respectful.

Bernard glared at Juline, "Whatst wrong with you. Canst you not cooperate? Dontst makest things worse."

Juline glared back at him and then back at the officer and then purposefully pursed her lips and folded her arms with mock resignation.

The officer continued, "We have checked his school record and its not good and reckless driving and a cold heart put him in no better light. This boy needs to be dealt with seriously," he said, looking searchingly at BJ, who gave him an iced look but did not respond in any other way.

"If we don't deal with him, he's going to be a problem to society," one of the other officer commented.

The other one who had not spoken before could not resist a dig, "Yes, these rich spoil kids are worse than the poor trouble-making ones, they do all kinds of things and expect to get away with it. That's just the point, your kind think that the world rotates round you. You think you can buy your way out of everything." He definitely had a problem with affluent people and thought nothing of wounding those in front of him, although he knew nothing about the parents.

Juline could not allow this jab to pass. "But, officer, we are not like that. Because BJ act a little impulsively it doesn't mean he is a bad boy. I am certain that when you were younger you did your little impulsive acts too," she defended, stressing her euphemism, impulsive acts.

The officer looked at her in a pathetic manner, turned away from her and then turned back. "Mother, you are fighting rotten for your son. What I might have done as a teenager does not excuse him. Wrong is wrong, whatever pretty term you might use to dress it up in."

The officer in charge called them back to the matter at hand. "Listen, let us deal with the problem as it is, what do we do with Bernard Junior?" This question ignited a discussion between the five adults which lasted a long time. Juline begged and pleaded for them to allow her son to return home. She proffered the arguments; that it was a first police offence for BJ and that sending him away was too drastic a consequence that would only result in the decadence of a brilliant mind, that could contribute a lot to society. Bernard Senior, despite a warning which came from deep inside, also pleaded with them to let BJ return home and back to school to continue his education. He did not feel right about what he was doing; but he consoled himself, he was his son and despite his bitterness about him, he deserved another chance.

The officer who had raised the point about spoilt rich children continued as if he had not been interrupted, "Most of you spoilt kids behave as if you can just do anything and get away with it! That's just the point; you think it is a part of your status! Driving away big vehicle, running through stop light and leaving your friend to die, that's just the point, think you are the axis, that's just the point, the very point I am making! He was very agitated as he made the point, and the table he was sitting around suffered an angry thump as he hit home the point.

"Tell me something, Father." The third officer faced Bernard directly and looked him straight in the eye. "How much time you spend with this boy?"

Bernard shuffled uneasily on the seat and averted the fixed look of the officer. He searched around for an answer in his mind but the search proved futile, "Well not muchst, you know youngst people alwayst busy withst their friends and activities at schoolst."

"So he spen' the whole day at school why you don't have time to talk to him?" the first officer questioned.

"No he doesn't," said Bernard, with a defeated look on his face, "but whenst he comest home he always gost to his roomst." His face revealed his embarrassment and those looking on felt sorry for him. The once vibrant, compelling figure was now a saddened shadow of manhood. Bernard felt like burrowing into a hole like a mole, but instead, he gathered a minute amount of strength and stared blankly at the officer. He did not look at his wife and son that would have taken too much effort and caused more embarrassment. BJ looked at him and saw the image of a cowering coward. He scornfully turned his head away and met his mother's brazen gaze, "Now here is a fighter," he thought, "my defender and shield, one who is not afraid of talking to meddlesome police officers." He flashed her a warm smile which she returned instantly.

The meeting ended with the first officer outlining certain rules. He told BJ to stand and like an army general shouting orders to his underlings he bellowed, "One, if you are caught driving without a licence again, we will see to it that you are not granted a proper licence for a few years when the time comes. Two, you are required to report to the station at least once fortnightly. Three, frequent checks will be made to the school in order for us to stay informed about your academic and behavioural progress, and four and last, if you step out of line and give your parents any more trouble, the state will be forced to make you its ward."

BJ's family cringed at the threat in the officer's voice, especially at the last pronouncement. In a way, Bernard was glad that some kind of regulation would be put on BJ's life. Since he was not physically able and his wife was against the idea of BJ not having his own way in everything, he was glad that some order, at least an attempt at order, would be in his son's life. Juline, on the other hand, was seething with resentment. How dare they try to make rules in her family when she was there and her son was involved? How dare they try to portray her son as a criminal, when he came from such a good home and was of such good breeding? Handsome BJ was her son and they were just envious of his good fortune, after all they were just police officers! Her son would achieve much more than that, soon everybody would read or hear of his prowess in whatever he chose to do.

Juline tried to strike some kind of compromise: "Officer I am certain that there is something my husband and I can do for you kind officers, if you let us handle this all by ourselves in our own way. We will deal with BJ ourselves and see to it that he stays right on track. Wouldn't we Bernard? And in exchange for your kind favour…"

"Stop there right now lady," said the officer in charge with command and shocked surprise in his voice. "What exactly are you trying to say lady?"

Bernard swung his head swiftly in Juline's direction and stared at her in disbelief. He hoped that his stare would silence her but Juline kept on going battery powered and programmed. "What I am saying is that we can help you, if you forget all of this and wipe those things about BJ from your book. We can…"

The second officer was now standing; his mouth opening wider by the second, some force inside seemed to be prying it open involuntarily. He gave Juline a thorny glare designed to put her in place and then he asked in an almost inaudible voice, "Woman you trying to bribe us? Is that the point? You trying to bribe three police officer in a police station! That is the point, you trying to bribe three police officer! That is just the factual down to earth point!" He walked of and spun around several times like a battery operated robot that had been wound up.

The officer in charge took over, "Will you all leave before I arrest this woman! Will you all leave at once?" His voice though calm had a cold, low freezing temperature about it.

The frost was transmitted to the family which made a hurried exit before the lawman could carry out his threat. No one spoke until they had driven out of the station.

"Juline you arrest a disgracest to this family. A terrible disgracest! How could I ever think you werest anything else but a woman seeking an easy ride on a roadst paved with gold? You are a sore disappointment." A tremor shook his lips, and he blinked angrily trying to resist the impulse to strike her.

"But look at you." Juline laughed back rudely in his face, almost losing her grip of the steering wheel. "Just look at you. You not even a man; you can't even take charge of your own child and home!" She was so angry that the steering wheel did a wobbly dance, and she almost ran off the road. She stepped on the brakes suddenly, almost capsizing the SUV. Bernard made a small scream as he relived the previous accident, which had made him lose control and command of his family and his life.

Juline steadied the steering wheel as the vehicle sought to make contact with the approaching wall. Nobody uttered a word as she righted the vehicle. Bernard had closed his eyes tighter than a bud and opened them only when the vehicle finished its sudden unsteady dance. Juline was breathing heavily, but Bernard did not glance in her direction. He could see BJ's composed, cold features in the mirror. He wondered if he had even flinched during the near accident. The boy's metallic exterior unnerved him when they stared at each other in the mirror. Bernard was the first to lower his gaze while BJ continued his silent, sinister stare in the silence of the vehicle.

CHAPTER 15

THE FAMILY FORTUNE DWINDLES

BJ continued school, seemingly complying with the police's dictate. He did not pay much attention to his father, even though he made numerous attempts to talk to him. Apart from a frosty good morning and good evening, there was no verbal exchange between them. As soon as Bernard entered any room that BJ happened to be in, the boy quickly departed, ignoring his father's "Wait, BJ, I wantst to talkst to you."

Bernard decided to leave him alone. Why should he force himself on a child, he had done nothing to him. One night after a day of excruciating pain, Bernard was somehow prompted to check his credit and debit cards along with some other important papers. He realized that one of his credit cards and two of his debit cards were missing. At first, he thought that he had simply misplaced them, but this was strange as he was always very careful with his financial affairs. After searching through everything he decided that something was definitely wrong.

Juline claimed she had no idea where the cards were, so Bernard decided to go to the banks to report the loss the following day.

"Good morning, Mr. Hemmings," one of the assistant managers at the First Bank greeted him after he was ushered into one of the inner offices reserved for special clients with special cases.

"Good morning, Mrs. Paige," Bernard responded, trying to sound cheerful. "How is business? I can see it is good, judging from the long lines outside," he supplied, answering his own question.

"Well, it is even better with you being here. You are always welcome at anytime." Her welcome flowed into her eyes and spread all over her face ending in a lovely smile, one that was either painted on or either came genuinely in that line of work.

"Well actually I am here on a different mission this time. I would like to report the loss of one of my credit and debit card. I just can't seem to find them anywhere at all in the house," he revealed, trying not to sound like an irresponsible child. His face had an anxious look on it.

"Well, that happens some of the time. When was the last time you used them in any form of transaction?" asked the assistant manager.

"Let me see," said Bernard, closing his eyes to aid his thought process. After a few seconds he replied. "I think it was about four months ago. That was when I bought some special equipment that the doctor had recommended," he added, certainty appearing on his face.

"Give me a minute and I will do some checking on my computer to determine the exact date," Mrs. Paige said. Bernard closed his eyes while he waited. About a minute later a sound of disbelief issued from her lips. "Mr. Hemmings, did you say four months ago?"

"Yes as farst as I remember, that wast the last time." He leaned forward, anxiously wondering at the strange tone of the assistant manager.

"That cannot be, Mr. Hemmings. Your debit card was used up to Friday of last week!" She turned to face Bernard, an incredulous look on her face. "The credit card was also used quite recently; as a matter of fact the last day of last month."

"I havest not been using those cards!" Bernard explained, aghast. "I havest not!"

"Well somebody else has been using them for you!" the outraged assistant almost shouted. "As a matter of fact, from the time you indicated until now, a little over a million dollars have been withdrawn!"

"What? Who? When? Where?" Bernard shouted, causing one of the workers next door to rush inside and another ran to get the security guard.

"It's all right, I'm not being attacked," Mrs. Paige told the worker, who was looking uneasily from one to the other. "We are just trying to unravel a mystery, a great mystery," she tried to explain and indicated for the worker and the guard to leave.

After reassuring themselves that everything was alright they withdrew uneasily, walking backwards and then turning full face around only to keep glancing over their shoulders furtively. Finally they disappeared and Mrs. Paige closed the door and turned to face Bernard. His face had become granite and still. She called his name but he did not respond. Life seemed to have left him suddenly. Mrs. Paige studied the face and despite the stony feature she detected pain and hurt. Hurt that made the tears long to escape but also froze them at the same time.

"Mr. Hemmings, Mr. Hemmings," she called, pity engulfing her as she looked at the splintered image of the once vibrant man. "Mr. Hemmings, I am sure that there is a logical explanation for all of this," she pleaded, trying to provoke a response. "Someone must have got hold of your cards and has been using them. You must find out who it is and get an explanation."

Bernard heard her as if from a distance. Despite his stony aura, his heart was contracting at an abnormal rate, threatening to tear itself from its mooring and overturn him. None of what Mrs. Paige said made sense to him, so much of his money gone! Digesting that reality choked him and he started spluttering. He wondered if he was going to sustain a heart attack, but mercifully he didn't.

Mrs. Paige was hovering around him, her maternal instincts ignited. "Mr. Hemmings! Mr. Hemmings! Are you alright? Do you need help? Do you want to see the doctor? Should I call for help? Speak to me Mr. Hemmings!"

Bernard stared at her speechless. She might have been a phantom, trying to make contact with a human being, but not being able to cross the divide into the real world.

He continued to stare at her and she at him. Then she started to call his name again, "Mr. Hemmings! Mr. Hemmings, speak to me!"

He still continued to stare, stupefied, shock registering in his face. Mrs. Paige's voice must have carried because the worker who had come to investigate the first time burst through the door, concern popping out of her eyes.

"What is it, Mrs. Paige? What is it?" she asked, running to Mrs. Paige's side. Mrs. Paige pointed to Bernard's face, "Look at him, I think he has gone into some shock or the other! He's just looking, staring without a word. He's not answering me; he's out of this world!"

Miss Belmont, the lady who was talking to Mrs. Paige was a little older than she was. She was a short, clean-faced woman with an experienced look about her. She walked over to Bernard, placed her hands on his shoulders and shook him violently. Receiving no response, she proceeded to hit him on both sides of his face. He made an angry sound and jumped up frightened. "Whatst! Whatst you doing?" He reached out at Miss Belmont and then pulled back his hands.

"Sit down, Mr. Hemmings," Miss Belmont commanded. "We were just trying to wake you up. You seem to have gone into shock."

Bernard stared at her, not comprehending for a while and then awareness dawned on his face and he sat down.

"Is there anyone that you would like us to call Mr. Hemmings? Did you come by yourself?" Mrs. Paige asked, anxiously feeling the need to speak to a family member.

"You can call my brother at this number," he replied, giving her a number. While Mrs. Paige dialled, he looked out into nothingness, a vacant look spread over his face and his eyes became huge and helpless like those of a child.

When Kenton, Bernard's brother arrived, Mrs. Paige appraised him of the problem. "What!" Kenton muttered, staring at Mrs. Paige as if she had told him that the sun would no longer shine. "I suggest you call the police right away! They will have to dig to the bottom of this mess and find the thieves. He or she must be caught and dealt with accordingly!" As he spoke his lips shook uncontrollably, slightly distorting his words and furious fire lit his eyes.

The police were called in, and after an avalanche of questions directed at Bernard and bank officials, the investigation started. Bernard felt as if his head would take off and leave the rest of his body. The headache which had started earlier at the back of his head, had now extended itself to every area. His forehead and ears were throbbing to an inner beat and his eyes felt as if they were being pulled inwards and then pushed out again.

When they left the bank, he told his brother that he was not going home, but would like to drive around for a while. He told him he wanted to think about things and what to do next, because he had a very good idea where his money had gone. Kenton disliked the idea of him driving around by himself in the state he was in, but Bernard insisted.

Bernard drove around not going anywhere in particular. The wind climbing in through the open windows of his

SUV calmed him somewhat and after a while the pain in his head subsided and he was able to think again. He had found out for sometime now, that he was not able to think clearly at times, especially after he had eaten at home. His thoughts would become cloudy and sleep would beckon to him. He had tried to associate this with particular food but discovered that the obscure thoughts came with just about any type of food. He had started eating heavier lunches when he was out and had avoided eating too much at home. Juline had noticed this and commented, "But, Bernard, why yuh not eating up as usual? You can't just waste so much food! Why a big man like you don't have any appetite after a whole day at work?" She watched his face closely as he answered.

"Ah really not hungry, I eat a big lunch each day," he answered, getting up from the table.

"Well, you better tell Miss Thelma (the helper) when you going to eat and when you not going to eat, so that she don't waste her time cooking so much food."

Bernard did not answer but went to his study. While he was watching the news a thought rushed into his head, he waited until he heard Juline going upstairs and then when he was certain that no one was around, he moved as stealthily as a cat hunting its prey into the kitchen. His dinner was still covered in different dishes because Juline had not bothered to put it away or give it to the dogs. He selected a small plastic container from an overhead cupboard and swiftly spooned a little of each dish into it. Afterwards, he rearranged the contents of each dish so it would look undisturbed. He smuggled the dish into the study and placed it in his case. The following day he made arrangements with his doctor to have it tested. He decided that he would call the doctor to find out what the results were as soon as he was able to.

As he drove around, his thoughts became unclouded. There could only be two persons responsible for the theft of his cards and his money. But why, why did they need money when they had enough to spend? Why were they trying to bring him down? Hadn't he done enough for them? He almost ran a red light so he discontinued the thoughts.

He pulled into a nearby shopping centre and bought some clothes and then he booked into a hotel for a few days. He would just disappear for a while and then decide what next to do. He would only answer his cell phone when he felt like. He was just too tired of everything; he would just give his devious family a few days break.

Afternoon hurried into evening and evening rushed into dusk and then tumbled into nightfall, and no Bernard. Juline dialled his cell phone until her fingers ached. Where could he be? Since he had had the accident, he had stopped arriving home late. She wondered if he were ill or had been involved in another accident. Anything was possible based on the volcanic eruption which had followed the discovery of his missing debit and credit cards. He had lashed out accusingly at her and had left the house spewing larvae in the form of swearing and threats directed at anyone who had misplaced, removed or stolen his cards.

She had not seen him since, but she had seen the police who had turned up at her workplace to question her about the missing cards. It happened just after she had eaten her lunch and had gone into her office. There was a loud, insistent knock on her door and before she could get to the door, it was wrenched open by the assistant manager who announced in a questioning tone that a police officer was at the front desk and would like to see her. "A wonder what happen now?" she added, scrutinizing Juline's face. Her look changed from questioning, to sympathy and then ended with a dubious wide-eyed scrutiny.

"I have no idea what it could be," Juline replied calmly, but this calmness was mocked by the chaotic swirling of ideas in her mind. "Please tell him to come to my office," she said, not wanting anyone at the front desk to overhear anything that would transpire to get into prying ears and fly out of malicious mouths.

She sat at her desk and waited nervously turning the pages of her daily planner, looking for nothing in particular. She knew why they had come and she was prepared. She was prepared to duel with them if necessary. She threw the planner aside and bent to retrieve it when it missed the intended spot and slid to the floor. As she bent to pick it up, she jumped back and a small scream freed itself, as a tiny frightened grey lizard wriggled onto the book and then vanished among the books on the shelves. Her scream was punctuated by a knock on the door.

"Come in," she responded lightly, trying to gain a measure of composure.

The door opened and a police officer walked in and greeted her warmly. She returned the greetings trying to match his warmth. She offered him a seat and then took one facing him.

The officer cleared his throat and began. "Mrs. Hemmings, I am here on a very serious matter." He stared Juline in the eyes and she returned the stare, unflinching.

"What serious matter officer? Has something happened to a family member?" she enquired, trying to force concern into her eyes and voice.

"Well yes and no," stated the officer, looking directly at her. "No if you are talking about injury or death, yes if you are talking about theft."

"Well I am relieved to know that everyone is okay," she said, slumping in her chair and looking resigned, "But what has been stolen?" she asked, her eyes showing new interest, "and from whom?"

"The bank called me in and reported that your husband debit and credit cards have gone missing." He paused to let his words soak in, watching her reaction all the time. She did not flinch nor unlock her eyes from his but gave him a steady stare. He continued, unmoved by the direct eye contact, "He is adamant that he had them at home so I must question both you and your son and the helper as you are the ones who have access to the home and the bedroom." He paused and looked at her again, her stare had not wavered. "You are his wife and I believe you share the same bedroom. Correct me if I am wrong."

"Well, we are married and have a relationship so it is very natural that I do," she replied, indignation beginning to steal into her voice.

"Oh good," he commented, "Well that leads me to the next question. Do you normally use the same cards? Is your account a joint one?"

"Yes we have a joint account but we also have separate accounts. If we need money from the joint account we normally tell each other before we withdraw anything," she volunteered. "I do not usually use his cards and he does not use mine," she continued, the stare unwavering.

"Good, but do you know anything about the other accounts apart from the one that you share?" the officer questioned.

"What do you mean know anything about the accounts?" she enquired, looking directly at him.

"Well, do you know the number of the account or the pin number?" he questioned again.

She hesitated slightly before answering. This was her first sign of hesitancy since the questioning had started and the officer noted it with great interest. "Yes," she answered, her self-confidence surfacing. "He knows mine as much as I know his. There have been a few times when we have done business on each other's behalf, so yes, we do know each other account and pin numbers," she furnished.

"Have you had an occasion to use his accounts recently?" he continued his inquisition.

"No, I've not," she replied quickly.

"Do you know where he keeps them?" he enquired.

"Well I do not know that he has any particular place in his room," she said.

"Have you started or joined any new financial venture recently?" the officer wanted to know.

"What do you mean financial venture officer?" Juline questioned.

"I am certain you understand the term, Mrs. Hemmings, but what I mean is, have you invested in anything new or have you started any new business?" he enquired, watching her keenly.

"I would have liked to but I do not have the money," Juline laughed.

And so the questioning had continued until he left. When he was gone, Juline sat for a while rehearsing the questions and her answers. He was a sly one. Her summing up was interpreted by the assistant manager bursting into the room to find out what was wrong. She appeared to be unsatisfied with the answer that there was a problem with her husband's business.

When Bernard did not come home by ten o'clock Juline called Kenton. After several rings he answered the telephone, his voice tired and sleepy. "Yes, who is this?" his irritation came through quite clearly.

"It's me, Juline," Juline replied. "Bernard has not come home yet, and I was wondering if he was with you or if you know where he is?"

"Bernard not at home! I left him from this morning, and he did not come over to the business. He said he would drive around for a while but that was a long time ago. He does not usually stay out at nights, not since the accident!" Kenton was now fully awake and concerned. "Let me see if I can get him on his cell and then call you back." He hung up without waiting for any comment.

"Much good that will do him cause I have been calling all his numbers non-stop and getting no answer," Juline remarked to no one in particular. BJ was presumably asleep in his room so she did not have anyone to talk to. She did not want to wake him to tell him about his father's absence because she knew he didn't really care. She wondered if he was really hurt or had fallen ill somewhere. She felt a tinge of concern for her husband, not the intense emotional surge she would have felt when the marriage was enjoying better times. Things had really gone bad for them, fate had somehow conspired with Bernard to destroy her happiness, only BJ remained of that former hope. She didn't care what anybody said, she loved BJ more than anyone else. He was the only person who made sense in this life.

The ringing of the phone intruded on her thoughts. She picked it up after the second ring. Kenton was at the other end, his anxiety carried over the phone as he spoke, "I am not getting any answer at all, I just don't understand, cause he never stays out at night anymore. He's just not strong enough for that."

"I can't make any sense of it either because he normally comes by latest six," Juline replied, beginning to realize that this was becoming serious. If anybody knew anything at all about Bernard, it was Kenton. They were only a year apart in age and were very close. Whenever there was a problem, Kenton was the first person that Bernard would call and that was why Juline had called him first. If Kenton didn't know where he was then…

Kenton was speaking again, "What I don't understand Juline, is why you waited until now to call and tell me this, when you know that Bernard is not well and that the timing is off." His voice had become slightly agitated and a hint of annoyance was evident.

"Are you trying to blame me for something Kenton?" Juline posited, ready for battle.

"All I am saying is that you took a mighty long time to contact me when you know the situation!" his tone was rising and was threatening to become a shout.

"You know what, if you hear anything call me because I am not in the mood to fight," she said, hanging up the phone abruptly.

"That woman is Bernard's worst mistake in this life!" Kenton shouted to the house as he started dialling other close relatives in search of information about Bernard.

"That man and his family are the worst things that ever happened to me!" Juline exclaimed as she went upstairs to her room, "always wanting to blame me for something. I just hate them!" She looked in on BJ who was fast asleep with the light, computer and television on. She quickly turned off the computer and television; but not before gasping at what was displayed on both screens. "Oh BJ, you are not supposed to be watching anything like that," she whispered more in shock to herself than the sleeping form curled on the bed like a semi-circle. "No my son, this is not good!" she continued in a whisper, shutting down the computer and turning off the television and the light.

As she prepared for bed, there were two thoughts occupying her mind.

CHAPTER 16

THE INQUISITION

Morning arrived with the sun laughingly distributing its rays all around. The trees, shrubs and flowers caught them and started stirring to life. The dew did not share their gladness as the sun, grinning wider now starting to suck the glistening moisture from the greenery. As if empathizing with the dew, a daring dark cloud came out of hiding and stalled the sun's action. The sun retreated for a while and then not to be daunted, it made a half-hearted comeback, fighting to restore its dominance but the cloud kept it at bay and both remained at odds until the sun gave up, overpowered by the cloud which poured its water over everything, merging with the dew and then suffusing the thirsty earth.

Juline and BJ were standing on the verandah waiting for a lull in the rain, so that they could go to the nearest police station to report Bernard missing. She was feeling sleepy, as Bernard's family had kept ringing throughout the night to enquire if he had come home. Juline had been tempted to turn off the phone so that she could get some sleep but feared to incur the wrath of the family. At five o'clock, Kenton had called and told her to go to the police station and he would meet her there. The rain had started just as they were getting ready to leave and Juline, who hated driving in the rain, had decided to wait until the rain had stopped or taken a break from its activity.

She had told BJ not to go to school as it would seem insensitive and she did not want to irk any of the family members. She was glad to have BJ's company because he was her only ally. She no longer turned to her side of the family for help, because they did not seem to be very supportive of her, especially in matters related to BJ. She had decided some time before, that she didn't need them, or her other so-called son as she had BJ.

She moved closer to him and together they watched the plants subsiding to the whims and fancy of the rain. As soon as one assault was over and they raised their heads they were beaten down again. Some aging flowers had been torn from their anchors and were being mauled by the element.

Juline broke the silence, "BJ, where you really think your father could have gone?" she asked hesitantly, knowing that Bernard was not BJ's favourite subject.

"I don't know and a really don't care," he answered, stressing the word care.

"BJ, despite everything that happen, is still your father, don't talk like that," Juline said in a slightly reprimanding tone.

"Why should I care? He doesn't like us, neither you nor me. A bet if he could put us out of here him would do it, especially me!" he retorted, venom seeping into his tone.

Juline did not answer right away; when she did it was with warning for BJ. "Yes son, but make sure that you don't make anybody realize how you feel, because they will want to accuse us of something if anything happen to him." She looked squarely at him, trying to make sure that he understood her. She continued, "The police came to my workplace yesterday."

BJ turned fully towards her, a questioning look in his eyes, "For what, don't is last night him never come home?" Misunderstanding showed in his eyes as he looked at his mother.

"They did not come about Bernard himself being missing, they came about his missing debit and credit cards." She stressed 'missing' and looked away from BJ.

"So why did they come to you about that?" he asked, his tone filled with derision.

"Well, they figure that since he reported that they were stolen from home, one of us must have taken them," she replied.

"One of us, they suspect me too?" he asked, as if this was unexpected.

"Yes, cause the officer said he would question you and Miss Thelma another time," she announced, looking deeply at him.

"How come you didn't tell me from yesterday?" BJ questioned, a frown masking his face. "How come?"

"You came in late yesterday evening and by the time I came to your room you were fast asleep. Then I went to sleep after dinner and then this whole thing began by the time I woke up. When I checked, you had obviously got up and gone back to sleep," she told him, hoping to appease him.

"How do you know I was up?" BJ wanted to find out.

"Cause you left everything on and then went into your bed," she said, averting her eyes.

BJ did not answer right away, then he said, "What do they expect me to tell them, that I stole his cards?" He made mockery sounds with his mouth.

"I don't think they will be asking any questions about that now, since this new problem has arisen, so don't worry yourself. Let us go now; the rain stop a bit." She touched his hand and led the way.

When they got to the police station, Bernard's family was already there. It seemed as if all of them had turned out to make the report. The look they gave them, spoke clearly of what they considered her tardiness in getting to the station. "It was raining heavily where we live," she offered, answering the unasked question. "I do not drive very well in the rain so I waited until it had stopped," she further explained. She received some glances akin to the weather, but she did not allow them to bother her.

"We have already lodged the complaint, but you can go ahead and speak to them," Kenton spoke up pointing towards an inner room.

Juline touched BJ, motioning him to go in front of her and then she followed. She went inside the room and spoke to an officer sitting at the front desk. He directed her to another officer who told her to sit. After filing the missing person's complaint, she went outside to where the rest of the family was waiting. She felt uncomfortable among them; from the look on their faces they somehow seemed to be blaming her for Bernard's disappearance. Well, let them blame on, she was just at bay as they were, she had nothing at all to do with his disappearance.

"Well," Bernard's father said, "What are you going to do now?" his nervousness was evident in the tremor in his voice. In addition to that, his face looked haggard and feeble.

"I suggest that everybody goes home and wait for news. I myself will go driving around the area I last saw him and I am getting some help from a detective who is on leave. The police will also be doing their own investigation; even though they are saying it is still early days yet for him to be declared missing. You know how they sometimes are, they want to be certain about something before they act."

"I have to clear up some things at work before I go home for the day, but I will drop BJ at school first." Juline announced. She said goodbye and took her leave, not looking back once.

After she dropped off BJ at the school gate, she drove away but not to work. There was somebody she had to talk to about an important matter before she did anything else.

BJ went to the first class and then decided to leave school. He eyed the school gate closely and when the guard had turned her back to open the front gate to let a vehicle in, he sneaked out through the side gate. He walked to the busy intersection and stopped a taxi. He directed it to his community and got off before he reached his house. He did not want to get off directly in front of his home or be identified if there was a problem.

He had a way of entering the house without anyone seeing him or without sending off the alarm. He had made preparations before he left home that morning. He knew exactly where the helper was because he could hear her singing, "Great is thy Faithfulness, oh Lord my Father." Her pleasant contralto, with its many dips and slurs, pervaded the house. He had locked his room before he left so she would not know that he was in there. But his room was not his objective just now. With his father missing, there were some important documents that he wanted to have in his possession and now was a good time to get them. He knew that his grandfather and uncles would soon be in charge of certain things even though his mother was there; so now was the opportune moment to get what he wanted.

Like a cat stalking a lizard, he stealthily went into the room and locked the door. He placed his ears on alert in case the helper stopped singing and decided to come upstairs. He searched drawers and a safe for what he wanted. He found a number of important documents but not the one he or his mother would have wanted. His countenance changed to a slight scowl as he contemplated the hiding place of that special document. It must be somewhere in the house! The thought came to him suddenly; that it could be in the safety deposit box in any of the banks which his father was a member of. BJ's scowl deepened and he blinked his eyes in anger. He must find a way because he could not allow certain things to happen to his mother and himself.

The singing stopped and BJ listened for footsteps. Hearing none, he replaced the documents because he did not want any suspicion to be directed at his mother and himself. When the singing started again, he went to his room and locked the door. He would go back to school later on then come home as if he had been out all day long.

For the entire day, there was no word from or about Bernard. BJ heard when his mother came in but did not show himself. He watched television until mid-day and then sneaked out the way he had come in. Again he walked down the road and then took a taxi back to school.

The following morning there was still no word of his father. Again, Juline went to the police station. This time she was told she could not leave as they wanted to question her.

"So now I am a suspect in my husband's disappearance," she said sarcastically.

"I did not say you were, but we have to question all close family members, all members," the young officer who was accompanied by a female officer replied. They told BJ to wait in the reception area until his time and then led Juline to a small, sparsely furnished room at the back of the station. Juline gingerly sat on the chair she was offered and made certain that her hand did not touch the cluttered, discoloured table. The room was old and needed painting. In some sections, the ancient paint in discord with the wall had loosened itself and had become detached, showing a steel grey underneath.

The female officer placed a tape-recorder on the table before speaking. Juline felt as if it were 'Law and Order,' except that she was not watching it, but was one of the participants on the wrong side of the law.

"Mrs. Hemmings, I must repeat that we are not accusing you of anything, but we must question everyone closely connected to Mr. Hemmings. Somehow, somewhere, we might be able to make a connection and solve this mystery." His voice was too loud and it irritated Juline but she knew she could do nothing about it.

"Yes I understand," she said, thinking that she didn't know why anyone would think she knew anything about her husband's disappearance.

"Well Mrs. Hemmings," the female officer began, looking directly at Juline, "when was the last time you saw your husband?"

"I already told you yesterday and my answer is the same, when he was leaving the house for work." She was annoyed that she was being asked the same boring question twice.

"Was he dressed any differently from the way he normally dresses?" the female officer continued, pretending not to see and hear the irritation on Juline's face and in her voice.

"If it was my husband I would be happy to answer any question," the officer thought, frowning inwardly.

"No Miss, just the same as he always does," Juline answered.

"Which was?" the officer continued.

"Long sleeve, baby blue shirt, dark blue pin stripe pants and black leather shoes." She answered, her boredom deepening. "Same clothes I told you about yesterday."

"Mrs. Hemmings," the male officer took over, "what is the relationship like between you and your husband?"

"What?" asked Juline, taken by surprise.

"I'm asking what the relationship is like. I mean how you relate to each other?" he repeated, talking loudly as if she were outside the building.

"I heard you perfectly well, and I am intelligent enough to know what you mean. What I don't understand is why you should be asking me that question?" She looked at the officer nonplussed.

The female officer spoke up, "Mrs. Hemmings, it was brought to our attention that it was only two days ago that your husband reported his credit and debit cards missing. In addition to that, he claimed that they were taken from his home."

"And not only that," the male officer interjected, "he went missing the same day he made the report," the echo of his voice bounced on the wall and ricocheted into Juline's ears.

"So because of that I am a prime suspect?" Juline questioned. "How do you know that Bernard lost his cards at home? And why would I need to steal from my own husband when we have a joint account?"

"We did not say you were the thief," the officer hastily replied. "It is our job to try and find out what has happened and to explore all avenues. It is obvious that there might be a link between the cards and his disappearance."

"Well, you can make any link you want to make but I am not responsible for anything that has happened." Juline folded her arms and stared at the officers, unruffled.

"You still have not answered my question, Mrs. Hemmings, what is the relationship like between you and your husband?" he repeated adamantly, refusing to let it go.

"We are just like any other couple, we have our bright days and our dark nights," Juline answered.

"How dark are your dark nights?" the female officer came in, seriousness written all over her face.

"We argue about some things, just like any other human being on the earth. Do you ever argue with your person or is it a heaven on earth situation?" Juline turned the question on the police officer much to her surprise.

"Well I suppose we do, but I will not discuss that seeing that I am not the one under scrutiny," she fired back, stopping Juline before she could use her as a shield.

"Mrs. Hemmings, how does your husband and his son get along?" the male officer continued.

"As well as any teenage son and father," Juline answered.

"That does not tell me anything at all," shouted the officer, the boom of his voice echoing all around. "Everyone knows that teenagers behave differently, some are quite passive, some are stormy, and some are in between. Is a no man's land for them. You tell me which part of that equation does your son and his father fit in?"

Juline cleared her throat; she was cornered like a rabbit. She knew that the police already had information about BJ and his father that could be easily checked, so she did not want to say anything contradictory neither did she want to implicate BJ in any way. "Well they did not usually see things from the same level but these days some things are more levelled," she replied, the vagueness of her statement coming across feebly unconvincing.

"Again you need to explain what you mean by 'level' and 'more levelled'. To me those terms are relative," the female officer responded.

"Well they sometimes did not share the same views about how teenagers should behave, what they should wear, where they should go, etc. but now they kind of meet each other half way about some things," she said. Before anyone could respond she added, "He behaves just like most teenagers, just like you and I did when we were his age." She ended, triumphant at being able to generalize matters in the defence of her son.

The officers looked at her carefully without answering for a while. This woman was clearly trying to build up a defence for her son. The female officer wondered what the boy was really like. She also realized that that information would not be forthcoming from the mother.

"Just wait here a while. I will call your son, as soon as he comes in you may leave," the officer said getting up and moving towards the door.

"Will he be questioned in my presence?" Juline's words halted the officer before he got to the door.

He spun around, a question in his eyes, "No, do you have any objections?"

"As a matter of fact, I have," Juline emphasized.

"Are you afraid he will tell us something you don't want him to?" the female officer asked, looking straight into Juline's eyes.

"We have nothing to hide, but I would prefer to be here when he is being questioned," Juline insisted. "I think I had better get my lawyer," Juline retorted.

"Why not hear what the young man says before you decide to do that?" the male officer advised, sensing the difficulty they were now faced with.

"I will call him and you can ask him," the officer said moving off.

He came back with a sullen BJ and put the question to him.

"I have nothing to hide Mother, they can ask me any-thing they want with or without you here," he looked defiantly at the officers. "You can go Mother; I will meet you outside when they are finished with me." For BJ, this was a long public speech. He said no more, but turned his back to his mother and waited for instructions.

"Sit down Bernard Junior," the policeman ordered, pointing to the chair his mother had just occupied.

BJ looked at him deadpan, wondering why he had chosen to call out his entire Christian name, which he hated so much. What was his mother thinking to have given him such a name from the Adamic era? He squirmed inwardly, thinking "This man really knows how to offend."

"Tell me, Bernard Junior, when was the last time you spoke to your father?" the female officer asked.

"Tuesday evening," BJ answered, having decided before not to furnish any details he thought unnecessary or too personal.

"What did you talk about?" the officer persisted, watching his face.

"I don't remember," BJ replied, returning his look.

"Do you speak to your father often?" the officer continued, hoping for a little more details.

"Yes," BJ lied, knowing the only talking that went on between them were grunted greetings. What would anyone want to speak to such a boring, hateful man about; who only wanted to tell you about your manners and how not to enjoy yourself as a youth?

"Do you normally go into your parents' room?" the officer asked, changing the line of questioning.

"Yes, all children do that!" BJ replied, looking at the officer as if he were stupid to ask such a question.

"Do you know where he keeps his private papers?" he questioned, not taking his eyes off BJ's face.

"No, I don't," BJ replied, realizing that they were trying to link the missing cards to his father's disappearance and that he was a suspect. Well let them continue with their questions he mused, all of this has nothing to do with me.

"Have you ever accompanied your parents to the bank when they were transacting business?" the officer continued his bombardment.

"Yes, when I was younger," BJ answered.

"By younger what do you mean?" the female officer joined the questioning for the first time.

"Maybe up to eleven, twelve," came the matter-of-fact reply.

"Bernard Junior, do you know your father's pin numbers?" the officer asked steadily, slowly, as if he were asking for his name.

BJ's heart did a fast flip; it certainly did not reflect the frosty weather on his face. "No, I have had no reason to use any of his cards so how could I know them?"

"Well you live in the same house, you go into his room at will, you talk to him often and you are his only son. This is something that causes most men to confide in their sons, who knows, you may very well know that aspect of his business."

BJ glared at the man in front of him; seeing only his hateful, harassing face, highlighted by his hypnotic eyes, eyes that riveted themselves on you, seeking to probe inwardly. Well let him wait, he would not answer that question in any form again.

The police, sensing his reluctance, did not persist with that question, instead they switched their attention to the disappearance. "How do you feel without your father in the house?" the female officer asked.

"It is lonely," BJ lied. If only they knew how he relished his absence! He wished his father would stay wherever he was, so that he and his mother would not have to be mindful about anything except for the prying police who demanded that he visited them regularly and tried to keep an eye on him. He wished that they too would go missing, missing permanently.

"Do you know any of your father's favourite places, Bernard Junior?" the officer asked, using his Christian name and saturating him with irritability.

"Well, he normally goes to his club, Vintage Vibes, play his golf at the Armandy Fields and visit his friends who have horses, but he scaled down all of that since his accident." BJ finished giving what almost amounted to a speech for him, since the beginning of the interview.

"Oh, that accident!" the officer exclaimed, "How did it happen, do you remember?" he looked at BJ, trying to read the cold, unshrinking eyes, but they yielded nothing.

"The police mentioned something about brakes failure," BJ casually answered, his nonchalant attitude suggesting that he did not want to dismiss the topic. How and why did they come up with that one, BJ asked himself. They seemed to have documented everything about the man, especially the unsolved. He had to tread carefully; these police were cunning and were ravenous for information.

"He came in and his brakes were fine, he went out and his brakes undid themselves," the male police officer commented, breaking up the lines as if he were reciting poetry. "Mystery seems to dog your father's life, always breaking it up."

BJ was not good at interpreting the English Language; still, he realized that the officer was playing with words to comment on his father's mishaps in an amusing yet serious way. The whole thing was not lost on him, especially 'he came in and the brakes were fine'.

The officer became serious and returned to his questioning, "Have you done any checking around to see where your father might be?" the officer peered at him as if he were near-sighted and could not see well.

"No, my father's friends are big people so my mother would be the one to talk to them, not me," BJ said, looking at the officer as if he had made a blunder.

The officer met his gaze without flinching and did a mental summary of the teenager, cold, calm and calculated, a youngster to watch, closely, carefully.

"You can go now, thank you very much for your cooperation," the male officer said, watching him until he went through the door.

"That one is the epitome of danger undefined," the female officer commented with a bewildered look on her face. "He's too everything that I can't put a label on."

CHAPTER 17

❧❧❧❧❧❧❧❧❧❧❧❧

THE CONFRONTATION

The telephone rang four times without an answer and then it stopped. It then started to ring hysterically for two more rounds. BJ wondered where the helper was and why she wasn't answering the telephone. At the fourth round, BJ heard running feet and then the telephone rested. A few minutes later, he heard the grill opened. He cautiously opened his room door, went out on the landing and peeped downstairs. Thelma, the helper, was opening the grill. She had a shoulder bag and an umbrella in her hand. BJ wondered who had rung the telephone and where Thelma was going. Well, wherever she was going meant a little more freedom for him.

He went back to his room and sat in front of the computer. Soon, he hissed his teeth and decided to go for a swim. He hoped no one would see him, as he was supposed to be at school. It was the fourth day since his father had disappeared. BJ was not in the least worried about him. Wherever he was, he could very well stay there and allow his mother and himself some time to themselves. Despite herself, his mother was becoming a little too concerned, coupled with this; family members on both sides were giving her the questioning eye. BJ was itching to tell them his mind.

He had not had a swim in days and he really longed for one so he went downstairs and around the back. He went into the pool room and changed into his gears. He decided to stay only ten or fifteen minutes, as he had to get out before Thelma came back and get back to school in time to be picked up.

The water was cool beyond expectation and BJ swam with much vivacity. He swam from one end of the pool to the other forgetting everything. He was lost in his elation and did not hear at first when a voice called to him. He finally heard a sound above the thrashing of the water and stopped dead in the middle of the pool. His heart turned upside down, righted itself and then turned in another direction again.

"And what might you be doing homest at this timest young man," his father drawled.

BJ looked at Bernard standing there with his stick in his hand. The water ran unchecked down his face as he fixed his father with a nefarious look. Without answering, he slowly got out of the pool. He picked up his clothes which he had placed nearby, in case he had to make a hasty escape and made his way to the changing room. He could hear the tap of the cane following him and wandered what he wanted.

"Why are youst not in schoolst young man?" Mr. Hemmings asked.

BJ did not answer, instead he commenced putting on his clothes.

"Is this what you do each day, pretendst to gost to schoolst and then comest home to have fun?" Bernard asked, scowling at BJ.

"What about you? What are you doing here? You finished pretending to be dead to draw attention to yourself?" BJ asked rudely, looking at his father now attired in blue jeans and sky blue polo shirt with blue and yellow stripes.

"Whost pretending to be deadest?" Bernard asked, staring suspiciously at BJ.

"You go away for four days without contacting anyone and then you turn up shouting at me!" BJ exclaimed, turning his back on Bernard. "Why you just didn't disappear?" BJ asked, turning his back on his father

"And letst you and your tiefing mother inheritst everything I workst so hardst for?" Bernard asked this quietly and threateningly.

BJ spun around as if he had been hit, "Who and which tiefing mother you talking about?" he enquired, his face suddenly breaking out in patches of red and his eyes blinking rapidly.

"Wantst me to repeatst? You and yourst tiefing mother, who tief my cardst and tief my money! Whatst you do with it? Eh, whatst you do withst it?" the anger and torment broke through his voice loud and serious like thunder pent up too long in the dry season and was about to unleash its wrath on the earth.

BJ heard it and was afraid, but he decided to face the fury, "Who you calling tief? Who you calling tief?" His voice was rising like waves in an angry sea, rising to meet his father's fury.

"Don't pretendst, you wretch, you well knowst what ah talking aboutst you an' you tiefing mother! Likest mother likest son, chip off the old block!" the thunder had broken and would strike any unprotected thing.

BJ's wrath spilled over, he turned on his father and struck him in his face, once, twice, thrice. Bernard fell to the floor and BJ ran from the room, then as an afterthought he turned back and picked up his wet gears. He looked at his father lying on the floor and ran out, wringing out the wet clothes as he ran. He went to his room and quickly changed into his school uniform. He placed the wet clothes into two plastic bags, placed them into his school bag and went out the way he had come in.

He got back to school and scaled the fence at the back. He heard the bell ringing and realized he had two periods left. He merged with the children going to class as if he had been there all day.

When class was finished, he walked over to the skip a little away from the school building and dumped a black plastic bag.

BJ's mother did not pick him up from school as usual, his cousin, Kachief, Uncle Fenton's son did.

"Where's my mother?" BJ asked, trying to look surprised when Kachief drove through the gate and beckoned to him.

"She's at the hospital," he replied, driving off.

"Hospital! Hospital! What happen to her, is she hurt?" panic rushed into his voice.

"Calm down youngster," Kachief said soothingly, "it is not your mother who is sick but your father."

"Father, how comes I didn't know that them fine him. How comes nobody call me and tell me!" BJ spoke with heartfelt concern, looking at Kachief all the time.

"Well youngster, this is just crazy, after everyone looking for Uncle Bernard, the helper find him right at home!" his voice had an incredulous chime to it which did not surprise BJ in the least.

"At home, what was he doing at home? Somebody bring him there or what?" BJ continued his innocent questioning.

"That is the mystery. Somebody call the helper and tell her to meet your mother at her workplace. When she got there, your mother told her she knew nothing about the call and she was to go back home." He paused with the story as he negotiated a corner. When he had successfully done so, he continued. "When she got home she saw your father's SUV parked in the garage. She was so happy that she ran into the house calling out his name." He paused again as the phone rang and he answered it. "Yes, yes dawg, me hear the news, as a matter of fact, Aunt Juline ask me to pick up BJ and tek him to the hospital so a dat mi a do now. Bwoy dawg, is a strange story, an' only Uncle B could a tell you what really happen but right now… Alright dawg, everything ripe. Later, dawg."

He drove on for a minute without resuming the story and BJ wondered if he had forgotten him so he said, "Kachief what happen after she go into the house?" his heart was sounding a gong and he tried to still it.

"Well she go everywhere in the house and she couldn't find him at all so she call the police and your mother and tell them what happen. After she call them, she continue to search on her own but didn't find him in the house." He paused again as the phone rang, interrupting the conversation like a troublesome child. "Yes daddy, yes sir, as soon as a drop off BJ a will bring it to mummy, yes sir, bye."

BJ noted the respect with which Kachief spoke to his father and contorted his face in disgust. He knew the two were close and had always thought that Kachief behaved like a child instead of a man around his father. Respect for father, what a pain BJ thought!

This time, Kachief continued the story without prompting. "She started to search outside and called his name, the constant calling alerted the dogs and they started to bark. Then one a dem run to the pool house and start barking and when the helper go in there she see Uncle B." He paused, allowing the significance of the news to settle in. He cast a furtive look at BJ to see his reaction.

BJ sensed that some emotional response was expected and so mustered a look of bewilderment, looked directly at Kachief and asked, "But how did he get there? A mean did somebody hurt him somewhere and then bring him back home? This is really confusing!"

Kachief did not answer immediately. He too was trying to process what had happened. After a while he spoke, "We were expecting to find him somewhere else hurt but he appeared at his own yard hurt!" his puzzled tone was the same as BJ's.

"How badly hurt is he?" BJ asked, assuming a tone of grave concern.

"Well, from what the doctors know now, his brain is severely damaged and he will be a vegetable for the rest of his life, unless a miracle happens." Kachief's voice held genuine sadness, because his uncle was one of his favourite people. He always thought that he had got more than his share of life's problem; what with that strange accident years ago and now this even more bizarre disappearance and reappearance.

Inwardly BJ was rejoicing; if his father was so badly hurt then he wouldn't be able to give any information about him, which suited him fine. He sat quietly for the rest of the way mulling over the events of the day and how his life would change. If only those interfering police were not around he could do practically anything he wanted.

At the hospital, there was the all too familiar scene of family members, police and well wishers trying to make sense of everything and hoping that they would awaken from what they wanted to believe was a nightmare. Only BJ's mother made a stir at his appearance. "BJ, I'm so glad you are here. Your father is not doing well at all. In fact, he has severe brain damage and we don't know if he will ever speak to us again. It is too bad, so sad."

She sounded genuinely worried, and BJ wondered about this. He did not ask any questions, he just stood there quietly with the others, shaking his head when he was included in a conversation but not really engaging anyone in the conversation. At one point he felt uneasy; it was as if he was being watched. He looked around surreptitiously and found his brother Jared studying him. Jared was serious and pensive. He regarded BJ disapprovingly as if he had caught him stealing or doing something wrong.

BJ glared back at him and the loathing was exposed. He had never been able to hide how he felt about his brother, his so-called successful brother; who had finished his law degree and was now doing the bar examination that would enable him to practise law. Jared stood tall and attractively imposing, he stood out even in the hospital among so many other tall attractive men. BJ wondered what he wanted at the hospital since it was not his father, and then he reluctantly admitted, that they shared the same mother and that his father had been responsible for him awhile. He was the first to avert his eyes and he could not explain the uncomfortable feeling that persisted. He shrugged inwardly and moved to where his mother was sitting.

After half-an-hour, the nurse informed them that they had to leave. She said one family member could remain behind. Of course, Juline, being the wife, volunteered to do so. When everyone was leaving, she turned to Jared and said, "Drop your brother home for me." Without waiting for a response, she turned and handed BJ the house keys and walked off.

CHAPTER 18

✤❧✤❧✤❧✤❧✤

JARED AND BJ FACE OFF

Raw anger churned inside BJ. Didn't his mother remember that he hated Jared? He would prefer to walk all the way home than to ride with his righteous majesty, what was his mother thinking of? It was now dark and BJ did not relish the idea of standing outside by himself waiting for a taxi.

Jared clinched the decision when he walked over to him and asked, "Ready BJ?" Without waiting for an answer, he strode out purposefully behind the others, not wanting to be left behind.

BJ stood for a while and waited until he had walked over to a silver Honda Integra and started the engine. He walked over and edged in slowly at the back.

"I don't think I'm going to bite you if you sit at the front," Jared's resonant voice came at him.

BJ sat where he was for a while and so did Jared who did not look behind him. He promptly got up because he reasoned that the sooner they got going, the sooner he would be able to get out of Jared's company.

He slammed the door viciously and the windows shuddered.

"BJ, tell me something, why you feel you have to damage other people's property? This isn't my car! I don't have money like your people to buy expensive vehicles, or to pay for damages on borrowed property!" Even though he was angry, his voice was low and controlled. BJ could not see his face but he knew that he was angry.

They drove for some minutes without any exchange between them. BJ looked outside at the scenery whizzing by. The city was alive with lights and activity. People were moving about lousily as if it were day. There were couples walking together, parents hurrying home, children still in their uniforms trying to get home and some people who were obviously going nowhere in a hurry, they were just sauntering along.

Soon, they left the city and entered the suburbs, the contrast was conspicuous; the only signs of life on the street were a few dogs who were socializing in groups. The houses seemed to be asleep as quietness pervaded. The lights were soft and subdued as if they were afraid of disturbing the occupants of the houses.

They took a shortcut through the hill and while they were climbing Jared spoke; his words were deliberate and measured. "So, BJ, your father is out of your way at last. You shall live happily ever after."

"What are you talking about?" BJ asked, turning suddenly in the seat, his voice matching Jared's.

"You know very well what I mean," Jared replied. "You fooled everyone but not me," he gave a low, cynical laugh which capsized BJ's equilibrium altogether.

"What you mean, I don't know what you talking about, since when we start talking?" his tone was riddled with scorn.

"Well, you quite right bout that, we never really talk! You always busy doing the talking and getting everybody's attention even when you were a baby," his sardonic laughter was not so low anymore.

"You just jealous because you never have a father and because mummy love me more than you," BJ fired back, gloating.

"That is so true, I was jealous and angry because I got punishment for things you did. Our wonderful mother punished me for many things while her son was praised. But guess what, fate or should I say God intervened and took me away from your manor on the hill so that I could have peace and become a better person," Jared furnished, his tone expressing joy which sounded silly to BJ.

"What better person, you are not any better than me," BJ's voice held scorn and ridicule. "You think you are the only one who can achieve something in this life? I am going to be rich and I don't have to sweat and study so hard and long," BJ's derision came through stoutly.

"When people work for what they achieve it is much better and more valued, than to gain things falsely or by hurting other people." The cynicism was gone from Jared's tone and it was replaced with sobriety. He added, "My grandmother by my father's side always say 'Mother have, father have, blessed is the child that have for himself."

"Jared you just jealous, cause nobody no have anything to give you! You would have hawked it up same like me or anybody else!" he laughed loudly and mockingly, hoping to stunt Jared's responses.

Jared had an agenda which he had to honour. "BJ say what you want to say, but I will make it with or without hand-outs. The important thing is the value of hard work. Anyway, I can hold my head up in this life, what about you?" He turned momentarily to see BJ, the light from the light pole illuminated both their features, BJ looked nervous. Jared was surprised to see that he had become so discomfited, that his face was glistening as if sweat would start running at any time. Good, Jared thought, I am making him nervous, I must be hitting very low and very close. "BJ, tonight you did not even seem to be a little bit sorry for your father!" Jared continued his attack.

"How you know that?" BJ fired back, angry at the observation.

"You look so composed and indifferent, it was as if nothing out of the ordinary had happened," Jared accused.

"You think that because you say you going to become a lawyer, you can go around accusing everybody?" BJ had lost his composure all together and was shouting now.

"You don't hear any accusations yet, because you think you fool everybody, but not me just listen to this!" Jared replied.

"I don't want to listen to anything you have to say, let me out of this!" BJ was angry.

"Well, I am not going to stop unless I have a reason to, so you can either jump out or keep your posterior still!"

BJ did not know this new Jared, the Jared he knew was the one who did what his mother said, or the one that would get the sad look in his eyes when he told on him and he was reprimanded or punished. He did not need to look outside to realize that if he jumped out, he would land several feet down the precipice, which hugged both sides of the road.

Jared knew that BJ would not attempt to jump out of the car so he continued talking. "You were always a spoilt boy, at first both mummy and daddy spoilt you, and then it was mummy when daddy realized what was happening. She made you get away with everything. She always had an explanation for why the son of her marriage was always in the right and other people were just jealous of his good looks and his amusing meanness! She made you what you are today, cold, calculating and devious!" Jared was definitely not out to spare any feelings, though he spoke without much malice in his voice.

"If we were not in this vehicle, I would send those words back down your throat!" BJ said, twisting around to face Jared. His voice had the hint of savagery, cold, hateful savagery.

BJ's tone did not jar Jared. "You can always fight me when I get you home, if you want to, but I am still going to finish my revelation of you. You started being evil since you were a child when you killed the neighbours' pedigree dog, tried to frame your sisters by stealing your father's own money and then planting the evidence in the girls' belongings." Jared's voice was without excitement; it was as though he was announcing the time. "You didn't stop there, because you did so many awful things at school and when your father realized you were getting way out of hand, you interfered with the brakes on his car." The last accusation was said in a low, very quiet voice.

"Find the proof. You live at my house? How you know. Maybe you are the one who did it because you're jealous 'cause our mother never married your father!" He was so indignant that he lurched at BJ but pulled back before he could attack him. The car did a dangerous sideway movement towards the edge of the road and Jared had to fight with all the strength and skills he could muster, to prevent the vehicle from diving over the precipice. When he managed to stabilize it, he parked it, clasped the steering and placed his head on it. There was silence in the car and outside, only the night creatures militated against the silence by continuing their nightly musical rendition, with their varied vocal instruments.

After a while, Jared turned to BJ who was sitting silently, an undefined look on his face. "If you want to fight me, I suggest you do it now." He took the key out of the ignition and stomped outside. BJ sat where he was, afraid. He did not know this Jared and he was afraid, really afraid for the first time in a long while. Jared seemed as if he meant business. Then BJ's stubborn streak returned, to shy away from Jared's challenge would mean he was guilty. There was no telling who Jared would share his accusations with and if he let him think he was afraid, it would be worse for him.

He flounced out of the vehicle, putting on a façade of bravado. He faced Jared but he could not see his expression very well in the semi-darkness but he sensed the anger. The only bright light came from the vehicle. BJ lounged at Jared the second time for the night but Jared was ready for him. He caught his hands in a vice-like grip and held on. BJ gave a gasp and tried to free his hands but Jared held on without effort.

"The next time you think about fighting me you would do well to remember I am a black belt and am moving up," Jared announced calmly. He allowed BJ to feel his strength and then he let him go suddenly.

BJ stumbled like one intoxicated and then fell backwards. He was very close to the precipice, and Jared felt real afraid for him. If he was not careful he would go over in his effort to get up. Jared wondered if he knew the danger he was in. for a while, Jared savoured the idea of BJ going over, it would be a relief to get rid of someone who had caused so much trouble. As soon as the thought was born, it perished, because Jared knew that he would now become the accused. Everyone who was at the hospital knew that he was taking home BJ and he would be blamed for anything untoward happening to him. He did not want to get caught up in what was happening in the family.

"Don't move, BJ, if you do you will plunge into infinity!" Jared warned.

"Why don't you just push me over?" the unexpected answer came.

"You don't know what you are asking and how will you get to spend the money you and Mom took from your father's account? I would not deprive you of that pleasure!" He walked over to BJ and looked down on him sadly, "My little brother, I have no proof but you are really on your way in destroying yourself and your family. I have no doubt that you are somehow involved in what has happened to your father. Isn't it strange that he was found injured at home? A very bizarre occurrence, missing for several days and then found at home. I suspect that he came home from wherever he was and for some strange reason you were at home and you two had it out and you did him in again!"

"It is really true that all lawyers are tiefs and liars. You certainly went into a profession that fit you, liar and trouble maker!" BJ shouted from the ground, his voice, sounding hollow and echoing all around. His words were thrown right back at him.

"I have said all that I'm going to say. You can say and do whatever you wish to. I have to be on my way." Jared extended his hand to BJ who laid where he was, he looked first at Jared, then he started twisting around but Jared's voice halted his action. "BJ stop it, you will go over!"

BJ caught the fear in Jared's voice and laid still. "Take my hand now or I will leave you right here!" Jared warned. BJ hesitated for a while, then extended his arm and Jared pulled him to safety.

CHAPTER 19

THE FLIGHT

BJ lay in bed bombarded by noises in his head. He had to make a decision and fast because Jared knew too much. Whether it was purely conjecture or some kind of facts, Jared could get him into real trouble. He did not know quite what to do because Jared was not someone he could get at easily, he was smart as well as strong and BJ had proven that. While he was musing, his cell phone rang. He looked at the number and saw that it was his mother. "Hi, Mom, what's up?" he inquired.

"BJ," her voice was filled with urgency and she spoke fast, falling over her words. "BJ, pack your things at once, at least important, necessary things, pack quickly!"

"What's wrong, Mom?" BJ asked, trying not to believe his ears. "What we leaving here for?"

"BJ, I cannot discuss this over the phone, the police on to us and we have to leave for a while. I will come in a few minutes, be ready. Pack your big suitcase and be quick!" She hung up before he could ask any more questions.

BJ lost no time in doing what his mother had commanded. The compelling quality of her voice and the word police propelled him. He chose his most fashionable clothes, sneakers and shoes and some of his small electronic games. No sooner had he finished packing than the helper knocked on his door. He went outside to her closing his room door behind him. There was no need for her to view his activity he thought.

"Mr. BJ, your mother say you should remember what she said to do. I leaving now to pick up the things she ask me to," announced the helper. "Your lunch on the table."

"Thank you," BJ replied curtly, not seeing the need for any more words.

The helper left and BJ continued his packing. He knew that her errand was just a guise to get her out of the house. His mother did not want her to be there when they were leaving.

Approximately five minutes later, he heard her drive in. She ran up the stairs hurriedly, calling to BJ as she did so, "BJ put your things in the vehicle and let's go!" she was almost out of breath and was panting as if she were being chased.

"But, Mom, you haven't packed so how we leaving?" he demanded not moving.

"I did that from last night," she replied, going to her room and returning almost immediately with a suitcase. "Let's go, time is against us."

She tugged the suitcase down the stairs without any words. When they got to the front door, she locked the door securely. As BJ lugged both suitcases through the front grill, he realized that his mother had no intention of allowing the helper to get back into the house, as she had taken no keys with her.

BJ sat silently beside his mother as she whizzed down the hill. The scenery ran past giddily as if it was glad to get out of the way of the fleeing vehicle. BJ noticed that his mother had taken a different route once they got on their way. It was the one they usually took when they were going far out of town. He thought it was time he had some answers. "Mom, you must have a good reason for all of this, where are you going?" He looked across at her, waiting for an explanation.

"BJ, you don't know but I kinda have a friend in the police force and sometimes I talk to him and even do him a little favour sometimes." She paused as she came to a fork in the road trying to decide which road to take. She choose the one to her left and continued to drive very fast. "Him call me," she resumed the conversation, keeping her eyes on the snakelike road, "and tell me that him get a big tip that the police know that we were the ones that took the money out of your father's account." She paused and allowed the information to soak in.

"But how did they find that out?" BJ was indignant and stared incredulously at his mother.

"The hidden cameras in the ATM machine picked us up," his mother said dully.

"But, Mom, you know all about machines, how come you didn't know that they could pick us up?" The surprise in his voice came through with a tinge of disbelief.

"I just did not take precaution a few times, but remember that most of the times we wore hats pulled over our faces. They must have used other things to help them when we were unprotected." She sounded burnt out, all the fire was gone out of her.

"So now because you didn't remember to take care, we are going to go to prison!" BJ sounded angry and frightened. "I am too young to go to prison. My whole life will be finished!"

"You will not go, that is why we are going to hide in the country. They will never find us where I am going," she tried to sound convincing but somehow it didn't quite reach her voice.

"I know all about prison and what they do to you there," BJ's fear was real. "Why didn't you buy tickets and let us go abroad instead? Why mother, why?"

"We will go eventually but right now they will be watching the airport so we cannot do that," she tried to sound cheerful.

"And you think they won't find us in the country?" BJ asked scornfully. "Where you know that the police don't know? Tell me that? You live in the town all the time and except for Aunt Lyn's house in St. Thomas, where else you know?" His agitation was growing, fear was smeared all over his features and his eyes were round like balls.

"I know of a place where no one would think of looking for us, not in a millon years," she announced triumphantly. "I ..." her next sentence ended prematurely as the unwelcome wails of police siren started in the distance.

"You don't think they are coming for us?" BJ shouted. "How comes they know we leave already. Yuh police friend must tell them about you!"

"I don't think so and I have no intention of getting caught," Juline replied, trying to keep calm in the face of danger. She turned off the main road into a small unpaved road suitable for smaller vehicles. It did not seem to go very far in and Juline drove only as far as she needed to. She just did not want to be detected.

As soon as she stopped the vehicle, two police vehicles roared by, sirens shrieking. BJ doubled over in the passenger seat, shivering as if he had suddenly been transported from the tropics to the arctic region and was not wearing proper clothing. Juline was braver; she turned around in the seat to stare at the radio cars. They did not slow down when they were passing her hiding place.

After the sirens had died, BJ remained doubled over in his seat. He jumped when his mother touched him. "Don't touch me! Don't touch me!" he stuttered, "You cause all of this!"

"But, BJ, what are you saying?" his mother asked, shocked. "What are you saying about me my son? I know you are frightened but this is me, your mother! I love you from before you were even born!" She moved closer and tried to hug him but he pushed her away violently.

"BJ, I can't believe that you are treating me this way! We in this thing together, and if we become divided we will only get into more trouble." Her voice was filled with disbelief and astonishment.

"You are the one who should be in trouble, you made me help you steal the money. Why did we need it anyway? Why? " the boy questioned his mother.

"BJ you seem to be turning an idiot. You don't remember what I told you ? I got the feeling that you father was going to change his will, give everything to the girls and then we would be out in the night dew, uncovered, wet, barely surviving; living like animals! You don't remember what I told you, eh BJ. You want to live like common people!" She was begging, pleading, trying to make BJ see reason.

BJ was past reasoning with her, "I am going to prison and all because of you. Mothers are supposed to guide children not lead them astray! You are the cause for all of this!" BJ was trying to contain himself but he had become hysterical. "Look where we are, eh, look where we are!"

For the first time Juline really looked around. She was close to a river, in fact, they were just a feet away from it. The brown muddy water was filled with debris of all description. The river was in spate and seemed to be in a hurry to fulfil an engagement downstream. The debris, at its mercy was battered and dragged along by its fury which was further announced by an incessant gurgling roar. Juline shivered as she looked at it. She had been in such a hurry to hide, that she had no idea she was almost in a river. The sparkling, gushing waterfall which added to the roar of the river held Juline's eyes only for a while as she turned back to BJ to try and appease him.

"Just look at where we are!" BJ shuddered, looking at the gnarled branches of the trees bending over the river as if protecting it. The trees were an uncanny green with healthy leaves which spoke of roots being nourished by the overflowing river. Some of the trees rose towards the sky, greeting it in their ascent. BJ did not like the look of the place, it only added to the low feeling he was experiencing. He couldn't bear the thought of being so close to her anymore so he opened the door and got out of the SUV. There was not much space for him to walk so he edged his way alongside the vehicle until he was standing in the road. He held his head and uttered incomprehensible sounds.

"BJ, you need to stop this. If we work this out together we can escape. We can go to the man who helping me all along to keep your father in place and the two of us protected," she edged up beside him and tried to put her arm around him, but he pulled away.

"Protect, protect who, then why we in this problem? He walked away from her. "You cause me to do bad things instead of helping me!" BJ looked furious as if he were about to hit his mother.

Juline was having the headache of her life. She could not believe that her son could be turning against her in spite of all she had done for him! "BJ, this is your mother! Remember me? Remember how I stood up for you all your life? What bad thing did I cause you to do?" she questioned, drawing close to him.

"I hurt him two times, not one, two times. I am sure the police will eventually find out and arrest me just like how they found out about the machine," BJ confessed, moving away from his mother again.

"You, you are responsible for what happen to your father BJ? You, how? I suspected you know about the first accident but the last one, BJ, my God, how could you?" she stared at him as if trying to recognize the fiend she helped to create.

"He knew about the money," he answered hysterically. "He told me so, knew that we both had taken it!"

Juline spluttered, "How, how did he know? That's why he went away. If the police find out about you, tell them he attacked you first. That's all you have to do, all you have to do!" She moved towards him and he moved away closer to the river.

"I would rather tell them you did it!" he flung the words at her, hoping to stop her from talking and advancing.

"You would never do that to Mummy, would you BJ, me who neglected everyone for you? I did everything for you my son, all for you," her pathetic voice rang out loudly, merging with the roar of the river.

She reached out towards him. He moved away again, hitting at her as he did so. In her attempt to dodge the blow she lost her balance, tripped and fell into the river. Although she could swim, she started shouting for help the moment she hit the water. "BJ help mummy! Help! Help! Do not let me drown!"

BJ watched her struggling in the water without moving. He felt bereft, yet a sense of relief came over him. She went down once, and then came up spluttering, her arms raised feebly like a bird that had broken its wings and was rendered useless. Her feeble attempts were mocked at by the swirling sweeping water which dragged her mercilessly into its depth. He turned towards the van and then a hand grabbed him and before he could react he heard a big splash. A figure jumped into the water. He turned around and faced the same police officer who had questioned him earlier. BJ wet his pants and stared dumbfounded at the officer.

"We were searching for you and we got the report that something strange was happening here. Some farmers spotted you and called the area police, so here we are," the officer said. "Here we are in time to rescue your mother and then take you both to jail! The rich and the ruthless. Why did you do it?"

BJ's horrified stare of silence did not answer his question.